A Miracle in Mexico

Orina prayed to God to save her and show her a means of escape from the man who had forced himself on her as her husband, before a Catholic priest and a priest of the ancient Indian Gods.

Juarez poured a strange, clear wine into a beaker and set it down beside her.

"On such an auspicious occasion," he said, "we must drink to our happiness."

He was speaking mockingly.

Orina remained silent.

She told herself that whatever Blessing she may have received from the Gods, she was now in the hands of the Devil . . .

A Camfield Novel of Love
by Barbara Cartland

S0-BMW-226

Dearest Reader,

Camfield Novels of Love mark a very exciting era of my books with Jove. They have already published nearly two hundred of my titles since they became my first publisher in America, and now all my original paperback romances in the future will be published exclusively by them.

As you already know, Camfield Place in Hertfordshire is my home, which originally existed in 1275, but was rebuilt in 1867 by the grandfather of Beatrix Potter.

It was here in this lovely house, with the best view in the county, that she wrote *The Tale of Peter Rabbit*. Mr. McGregor's garden is exactly as she described it. The door in the wall that the fat little rabbit could not squeeze underneath and the goldfish pool where the white cat sat twitching its tail are still there.

I had Camfield Place blessed when I came here in 1950 and was so happy with my husband until he died, and now with my children and grandchildren, that I know the atmosphere is filled with love and we have all been very lucky.

It is easy here to write of love and I know you will enjoy the Camfield Novels of Love. Their plots are definitely exciting and the covers very romantic. They come to you, like all my books, with love.

Bless you,

Barbara Cartland

CAMFIELD NOVELS OF LOVE
by *Barbara Cartland*

A NEW CAMFIELD NOVEL OF LOVE BY

BARBARA CARTLAND

A Miracle in Mexico

JOVE BOOKS, NEW YORK

A MIRACLE IN MEXICO

A Jove Book / published by arrangement with
the author

PRINTING HISTORY
Jove edition / September 1991

ISBN: 0-515-10672-0

Jove Books are published by The Berkley Publishing Group,
200 Madison Avenue, New York, New York 10016.
The name "JOVE" and the "J" logo
are trademarks belonging to Jove Publications, Inc.

PRINTED IN THE UNITED STATES OF AMERICA

10 9 8 7 6 5 4 3 2 1

Author's Note

GEOGRAPHICALLY Mexico is a unique country. It has towering mountain ranges, broad high plateaux, and jungle lowlands.

The temperatures are as varied as the scenery. Rainfalls in some places are a few drops a year. In the Southern part of the country the annual precipitation can be as much as sixteen feet in the Grijalva River valley.

Mexico has had roughly twenty centuries of turmoil, invasion, occupations, and revolutions. Spanish is the language now, after the Spanish Invasion, although English is widely spoken.

In some outlying areas the ancient Indian languages are still spoken by the inhabitants.

The God Quetzalcoatl is the God of Life, the God of Rain, and the God of the Morning Star, and has always been of great importance with the Mexicans.

Towns were built in his honour and the Marriage Service which I describe in this novel still takes place among his followers.

Benito Juarez was born a poor Zapotec Indian who was educated in a Convent-School, and rose to the Supreme Court. He became President, but once lived in exile in New Orleans.

There are many monuments to him, and because he was a great reformer known for his personal integrity and great ideals, he tried to lead his country forward to a new Nationalism.

Juarez initiated the Reform Movement which expropriated Church properties, placed education under state control, and proclaimed religious liberty. In general, he separated the Church and the State.

It took years to accomplish, but because of Juarez, the convent-educated Indian intellectual, it all began. What he did accomplish was to give Mexico a sense of Nationhood.

A Miracle in Mexico

chapter one

1889

"IF you will not marry me I shall kill myself!"

The young man spoke dramatically and walked across the room to stare out of the window onto Fifth Avenue.

Orina Vandeholt, who was sitting on the sofa, stiffened.

"Really, Clint," she said, "how can you talk such nonsense!"

"It is true," he said. "I have loved you for months. I have begged you a hundred times a day to marry me. But now I have come to the end. I can go on no longer!"

He was being so theatrical that Orina rose from the sofa.

"If you talk like this," she said, "I am going to leave you."

"No, no, listen to me! I love you! I love you! I cannot live without you."

She looked him up and down.

He was, in fact, a presentable young man.

At the same time, there was something a little unbalanced and weak about him which she disliked.

She did, in fact, dislike most men.

Since they had pursued her relentlessly for the last two years, she had become more and more fastidious and difficult to please.

There was always something about men who threw their hearts at her feet that she felt was wrong.

She could not put it exactly into words.

Yet she shrank from the way they spoke and the way they grasped at her.

She had emerged from the School-Room having been strictly brought up by English Governesses and English Tutors in an English home.

She had known nothing about men and very little about the Social World.

Her mother, Lady Muriel Loth, the daughter of the Earl of Kinloth, had been swept off her feet by an American during her first London Season.

It had never entered Lady Muriel's father's or mother's head that any daughter of theirs would consider a man who had crossed the Atlantic as a suitable husband.

In fact, Dale Vandeholt had been tolerated in England simply because he was extremely rich.

As it happened, he was also outstandingly intelligent.

He had come to England with some original ideas regarding machinery, railways, and ships which had intrigued everybody to whom he talked.

That included members of the Aristocracy, and even the Prince of Wales himself.

Vandeholt was an extremely good-looking, personable young man.

Yet it had never crossed the minds of the parents of marriageable daughters that he might be a suitor.

Lady Muriel had known the first time she saw him that he was different from any other man she had ever met.

Her father had given a large Ball for her the previous Season when she had been presented at Court.

After that, every hostess sent her an invitation to theirs, and she had been an outstanding success.

She was a very beautiful, quiet, gentle, and amenable young woman.

It had, therefore, astounded the whole family when she declared she was going to marry Dale Vandeholt.

In fact, she insisted upon doing so.

Her father had raged at her and her mother had cried.

Her relatives had sneered at him and pleaded with her.

Muriel just persisted in her determination to marry the man she loved.

If her father continued his opposition, she said, then she would run away.

"Running away" in this instance was not a question of going to Gretna Green or another part of the British Isles.

It meant going across the Atlantic!

Finally the Earl capitulated.

Grudgingly, and arguing with her father all the way to the Church, Lady Muriel was married at St. George's in Hanover Square.

Afterwards she and Dale Vandeholt left for New York.

Despite everybody's misgivings, the marriage had proved to be a blissfully happy one.

Dale Vandeholt was a far more civilised person than the English imagined he would be.

To begin with, his grandfather had been a Dutchman who had emigrated to America.

His mother was a very beautiful and well-bred Hungarian.

Her father had been the Hungarian Ambassador to the United States of America.

Like Lady Muriel, her mother-in-law had fallen in love and nothing could persuade her to return home to her own country.

Dale Vandeholt, therefore, had the brains of his father and the charm of his mother.

Besides what he had learnt in the land of his birth—a forceful drive.

This made him invariably get his own way.

He wanted Lady Muriel, and there was something between them that could not be translated into words.

Because he was determined to prove himself as wonderful as his wife thought him to be, Dale

Vandeholt climbed so swiftly up the ladder of success that anyone watching him was left breathless.

Everything he touched seemed to "turn to gold."

When finally his land in Texas was found to contain oil, his wife had laughed.

"Now you have everything, my darling," she said, "and you really cannot ask for more."

"Everything I have is due to you," her husband answered. "You wanted me to be a great man, and that is what I have tried to become."

He kissed her and knew as he did so there was no reason for her to answer.

She had always believed in him, and it was that belief that had spurred him on from peak to peak.

Or, rather, because it was America—from skyscraper to skyscraper.

Any sadness, if there was one, was because, after their first child, a daughter, was born, the doctors said that Lady Muriel should not have any more.

"Another child would kill her," they said to her husband.

Dale Vandeholt would have liked a dozen sons.

Because it was impossible, he forced himself to be content with his daughter, Orina.

Then tragedy struck.

When Orina was only ten years old, Lady Muriel died.

It was peritonitis, for which there was no known cure, and no operation had yet been discovered to prevent the victims from dying quickly but painfully.

Dale Vandeholt was heart-broken.

He felt that everything he had striven for was worthless compared to the loss of his beloved wife.

It would be true to say that if he had a choice of being penniless and having Lady Muriel with him, he would not have hesitated.

Lady Muriel's father, who was not yet an old man, then wrote to him with a proposition.

He said:

> Without anybody to guide my grand-daughter, Orina, I think it would be in the child's best interests if you would allow her to be educated in England, at least for some months of the year.
>
> I am sure Muriel, if she was alive, would want her daughter to have the grace that is perhaps a little lacking in such a new country as yours, and also that she should meet members of the family with whom Muriel grew up.
>
> They will be her friends, and, of course, prospective husbands when she makes her debut . . .

Dale Vandeholt knew exactly what his father-in-law was saying.

He was implying in a not very subtle manner that it would be a mistake for his daughter to marry an American, and that one in the family was quite enough.

Over the years the Earl had become reconciled

to the fact that his daughter was ecstatically happy.

Also every year her husband became richer and more important in his own country.

Dale Vandeholt was very intelligent, which was rather different from being just clever.

When he thought it over, he knew the reason why he had loved his wife so deeply. It was that she was so different from the rather brash, hardvoiced American women.

He had always found them lacking in the polish and what the Earl called the "grace" that was to be found in England.

Making what was a supreme sacrifice on his part, he sent Orina to her grandfather, but only after making it clear that she would spend at least two months of any year with him.

The Earl was overjoyed.

He missed his daughter and he was insular enough to think that however rich she might be, she had lowered herself Socially and personally by marrying an American.

Orina had enjoyed living in her grandfather's ancestral home in Huntingdonshire.

It was an extremely fine house with a large Estate, and she quickly learnt to appreciate the pictures on the walls.

Also that all the treasures which the house contained were part of the family history.

She was astute enough to realise that the antiques which packed the Drawing-Rooms on Fifth Avenue were slightly out of place in those heavy brownstone houses.

They also managed somehow to appear alien to their surroundings.

She thought they also seemed to look disdainfully down on their owners because they had acquired, rather than inherited, them.

She saw both sides of the Atlantic.

While she appreciated the bustle and "go" of New York and the fact that her father always had something new to show her, she also liked the serenity of England.

Everything was well-ordered and gracious, slower and calmer.

She would watch her grandmother receiving her guests with unhurried dignity.

It seemed to her like the movements of a ballet.

She watched the servants at mealtimes, never making a mistake yet performing their duties as if some unseen voice directed them.

The guests themselves, she noticed, behaved in a very different manner from the noise and chatter of Americans.

There the conversation took place across the table more often than to those on their left and right.

At the same time, she thought her father's horses on his Ranch more spirited than those she rode in England.

She did not tell her grandfather so.

But she knew the difference in their breeding and training.

It was a double-sided education which was certainly different from any other girl of her age.

In both countries she had the best of everything.

Her grandfather was a rich man, but her father insisted on paying for everything she required.

He sent her to England with an embarrassingly large Bank Account on which she could draw whenever she pleased.

Because her grandfather had pleaded that she should have her first Season in London, she was presented at Court by her grandmother.

She was taken to Ball after Ball.

She sat in the Royal Enclosure at Royal Ascot Races, and was undoubtedly, although it seemed unfair, the most beautiful girl of the Season.

It was, of course, not only her beauty which made her receive proposal after proposal of marriage.

The stories of her father's fortune and the fact that she was an only child lost nothing in the telling.

Orina would have been less than human if, by the end of June, she had not had a very good appreciation of herself.

It was then on her father's orders that she sailed for New York.

She was attended by a Chaperone, a Courier, and a Lady's-Maid.

The very best Suite on the ship was put at her disposal.

Her father met her in New York, and there were as many Pressmen waiting to photograph her as if she had been Royalty.

Dale Vandeholt had already arranged the most

enormous Ball which New York had ever seen.

He gave a dinner for nearly three-hundred people before it took place and a number of other guests came in afterwards.

Everybody present received a gift which was made of gold and that was embellished with Orina's initials.

There were three Orchestras to play for the dancers.

One was the best-known and most-sought-after in the whole of New York.

The second was a Gypsy Band which had been brought specially from Hungary for the occasion.

The third, which played country music, came from the Vandeholt Ranch.

They had been practising for a year to be good enough for this special occasion.

It was a party that was talked about in New York for a long time.

It produced everything unusual that Dale Vandeholt had ever heard about in the past.

There was a fountain which sprayed perfume and a lake specially created in the garden on which there were gondolas.

There were midnight fireworks which flared up into the sky.

It was a more expensive and dramatic Exhibition than had ever been seen before.

Not surprisingly, Orina enjoyed herself.

In the months to come she received even more proposals of marriage than she had in London.

Then, with a swiftness of mind that was like her father's, she decided she had had enough.

"Let us go to the Ranch, Papa," she pleaded.

He laughed.

"And leave all your admirers behind?"

"They all say the same thing," Orina replied, "and while their eyes look at me with admiration, their brain is adding up how much money you must have made last year!"

Her father had thrown up his hands.

"A cynic at eighteen? I do not believe it!"

"I am not cynical," Orina said. "I am just practical like you, Papa. It is better to face things as they are than to believe in Fairy Stories."

To her surprise, he did not laugh, but looked at her seriously.

"Fairy Stories do happen," he said quietly, "and when I met your mother, as far as I was concerned, mine came true."

"I know that, Papa," Orina said gently. "I can remember Mama saying how wonderful she thought you were. The moment she saw you, her heart turned a somersault."

She made an expressive little gesture with her hands.

"Unfortunately, that has never happened to me."

"It will happen," her father said, "I promise you it will happen to you one day, and that is why I want you to promise me that you will never marry any man unless you love him and also be quite certain that he loves you for yourself."

Orina nodded, and her father said:

"I have always known it was a mistake that you were an only child, but as God gave me so much in my life, I could not be greedy and ask for more. At the same time, as far as you are concerned, it is a great responsibility."

"I know that," Orina said.

"It is not only the responsibility for other people," Dale Vandeholt went on, "it also means, my precious, that as you already know, you have to separate the chaff from the wheat—and that is a very difficult thing to do."

Orina sighed, and, when she did not speak, after a moment her father looked at her sharply.

"If you have discovered that already, it has not hurt you, has it?"

"No, of course not!" Orina said quickly, too quickly.

She did not say any more, and Dale Vandeholt was sensible enough not to try to force her confidence.

They had gone to the Ranch, and he was happier than he had been at any time since his wife died.

They rode together, and they talked late into the night.

Then one evening after dinner he began to tell her his plans for the future and the different businesses in which he was engaged at the moment.

He was sensible enough not to expect to do everything himself.

He had scoured the country for eager young men to appoint as Managers.

They had, he believed, the same intuitive sense of what was right and what was wrong as he himself had.

He then went on to tell Orina his secrets, night after night.

She found herself thrilled and intrigued by the huge network he was spreading all over America.

"This is a great country—a new one!" her father said. "The opportunity for development is just waiting for able brains and able minds."

"That is why America is lucky to have you, Papa."

"I am very proud of what I have achieved so far," her father answered. "At the same time, there is room for everybody. There is no need for anyone to envy me when they are crying out for more Americans who are not only concerned with building and developing for themselves but also for the Nation."

He showed Orina his plans for the development of the railways which, he explained, were still in their infancy.

He had factories making machinery of every sort in a great number of the large cities.

He had sent men he trusted to Europe to spy out new ideas.

They were also to bring back men who would like the chance of putting the new ideas in their brains into action.

"You are very, very clever, Papa!" Orina said in awestruck tones.

"That is what you will have to be in the future," her father said quietly.

She stared at him.

"Do you expect me, if anything happens to you, to carry on with all of this?"

"Of course!" he said. "It is your destiny, and that is what has to be done, otherwise I shall have lived in vain."

Orina put her arms round his neck.

"You are still a very young man, Papa," she said. "I need not worry my head about losing you yet. But, of course, I would like to understand more and to do exactly what you want."

Dale Vandeholt kissed her.

"It does not seem fair, my precious," he said, "that you should have both beauty and brains. At the same time, the latter are very important where I am concerned."

They had stayed for a while at the Ranch before he had taken her on a tour of his great possessions.

They travelled on his own railway to Chicago and to many places in the West.

Then they had gone to Washington, D.C., and on to Miami.

He had taken her there particularly in order to show her some of his interests in ship-building and his yacht which was near completion.

It looked almost as big as one of the Transatlantic liners.

Dale Vandeholt was determined to have every gadget that no one else had.

He also had an engine which could out-speed any yacht already at sea.

Orina found it very exciting, in fact, far more so than dancing at a Ball or attending the large Receptions which were given for her father in every city in which they stayed.

The year was passing, and it was time to go back to New York.

It was then that Orina suggested they should first go to the Ranch.

"I want to ride one of your really spirited horses, Papa," she said, "which is very different from trit-trotting in Central Park!"

Her father had laughed.

"Very well, dearest, that is what we will do, although you may find it rather cold."

Orina smiled at this.

Her father had shown her the new heating system he had installed when they had last been at the Ranch.

It was different from anything she had seen before.

He had turned it on for her benefit.

It had made the Ranch house, which was a large one, unbearably hot.

She had thought then that when Winter came, although it might be cold outside, she would certainly not feel anything inside but the heat of Summer.

They had gone to the Ranch and spent Christmas there.

Her father had given her a necklace of perfect Oriental pearls besides a number of other gifts that would have been acceptable for any Queen.

Orina had been more delighted, however, to ride the obstreperous, only partially-trained horses.

Her father had bred them from the very finest Stud available.

Their time had nearly come to an end and they

had to leave for New York the following day.

They had gone out riding together.

It was very cold and there had been a sharp frost the night before.

"The gallop will soon warm us up," Dale Vandeholt said.

"I will race you," Orina answered.

They set off at a tremendous pace.

Then, just as she was thinking she had beaten her father and was well ahead of him, she heard him give a cry.

She heard a crash.

It took her some time before she could turn her horse and go back to him.

It was then she saw with horror that the Stallion on which her father had been riding had slipped on some ice.

The animal had fallen, and, as he did so, had rolled on top of his rider.

Orina managed to find help.

Dale Vandeholt had been carried back to the Ranch.

A large number of bones in his body were crushed and he never regained consciousness.

Her father's death made Orina feel as if her world had come to an end.

All she wanted to do was to stay quietly at the Ranch, but that was impossible.

Friends, relatives, and the Directors of his vast possessions all insisted that she should go back to New York.

When she got there she found he had left her everything he possessed. There was an enormous amount of work for her to do.

It was not only a question of signing documents, nor of simply agreeing to what were the obvious procedures that must take place.

It was also a question of direction and choice.

Dale Vandeholt had never imagined for a moment that he would die so young.

Yet he had appointed the best Attorneys and also the best Advisers to look after his possessions.

It was this company of men to whom Orina knew she could turn and rely on in the future.

She appraised them in the same way that her father would have done.

She discovered perceptively their strong points and their weaker ones.

Mercifully the Social World at first left her alone.

But, as the months passed, it all began slowly and relentlessly to take up a great part of her time.

At first there were just friendly visits of two or three people who had loved her mother.

They were eager to befriend a "poor orphaned child."

But the number expanded and expanded.

After six months in mourning, it was impossible to refuse everything with the old excuse that she wished to be alone.

A luncheon-party here, a dinner-party there, had soon developed into very much bigger occasions.

She knew she was being fêted not only for herself, but also for her money.

She was the most important as well as the richest

girl in the whole of American Society.

It was impossible for her not to become cynical.

Too many young men proposed marriage almost as soon as they met her.

They persisted in forcing their attentions upon her.

However much she tried to protest that she wished to remain single, they would not listen.

"I love you and I will make you love me!"

How often she had heard those words!

She began to think that they haunted her.

She heard them in the wind blowing outside the windows, in the creak of the stairs, and in the sound of a door opening.

"I love you! I love you!"

Sometimes the voice that spoke sounded sincere.

All too often she could hear the desire for gold behind the tone and see the glint of it in the eyes which gazed at her.

It was at night that she told herself bitterly that now no one would ever love her for herself.

Her mind would then go back inevitably to the incident that had happened in London during her first Season.

She had tried not to think about it.

Yet, when a man begged: "Will you marry me?" another voice much stronger was saying something very different.

It was a relief to attend a number of meetings and get away from her suitors.

Now she was having to cope with the most persistent of them—Clint Hunter—who was threatening to kill himself.

She looked at him as if for the first time.

She knew that if he went on beseeching her for a thousand years, she would never marry him.

"Now, listen, Clint . . ." she began.

He swung round from the window with a fanatical expression in his eyes.

"I know what you are going to say," he shouted, "and I am not listening! If you will not marry me, I will kill myself—but, by God, I will kill you first! You are a Temptress, a Temptress, a Siren! You attract men with your beauty only to damn them into an eternal Hell when they can no longer live without you."

He drew a pistol from his pocket.

"If I kill you," he said, "no other man will have to suffer as I have suffered!"

"Please, Clint, please, be sensible!" Orina pleaded.

He was pointing the revolver straight at her, and she wondered what she should do.

"Give me that," she said quietly, "and let us talk about this."

"There is nothing to talk about—nothing to say!" Clint shouted.

The hand pointing the lethal weapon at her shook.

Then, as she paused, wondering desperately what to say, he turned his arm round.

Pressing the barrel against his chest he pulled the trigger.

There was a deafening explosion.

Then, very slowly, Clint Hunter collapsed onto the floor.

chapter two

STANDING on the deck as the yacht moved out of port, Orina thought she had escaped.

From the moment that Clint Hunter had fallen to the floor, she had thought she was living in a nightmare.

She imagined he was dead.

When the servants came running, they found he was alive, but injured above the heart.

It was a wound which was bleeding profusely.

He had been carried off to Hospital.

When he had gone, Orina faced the fact that she was in a dangerous situation.

She knew what a story the Newspapers would make of it once they knew what had happened.

She was, however, fortunate in having her father's right-hand man in the house.

He was middle-aged and had been with Dale

Vandeholt ever since he had taken over his father's possessions.

When Bernard Hoffman came into the room where Orina was waiting for him, he saw she was very pale.

"Now, listen to me, Orina," he said, "this is serious, and we have to be smart about it."

"I have been thinking that already," Orina said. "Oh, please . . . help me! I had no idea this could happen in such a horrible manner!"

Bernard Hoffman smiled.

"It is the penalty of being beautiful," he said, "and also, of course, extremely rich."

"I know . . . I know," Orina cried, "but that does not make things any better, and you know people will assume that I drove him into attempting to kill himself."

"In a way that is true," Mr. Hoffman said quietly, "but what we have to do is to make everybody believe that it was a shooting accident, and had nothing to do with you."

"How can that . . . possibly be . . . believed?" Orina asked.

"I have told the servants," Mr. Hoffman replied, "that you were out of the room when it happened. You were next door looking for something you had been discussing together—a book or a letter—it does not matter. When you heard the shot, you ran in to find him lying on the floor."

Orina nodded.

"He had already shown you," Mr. Hoffman went on, "the revolver he had recently bought,

22

and because it was the latest model, he was very proud of it."

He looked at her to see if she was listening before he went on:

"It is of a type that is difficult to know exactly how many bullets have been fired, and he therefore miscalculated in thinking it was empty when in fact there was one shot left."

Orina understood exactly what Bernard Hoffman was telling her.

She sank down in a chair, realising that, strangely, and it was very unusual for her, she was trembling.

"Now, what I think you should do," Bernard Hoffman was saying, "is to disappear from New York."

"Will not people think that heartless?" Orina asked.

"Maybe your immediate friends will do so," he replied, "but I am thinking of the newspapers and those tiresome, inquisitive, and very suspicious Journalists."

"Then of course I will go away," Orina said.

"It is a journey that has been planned for some time," Mr. Hoffman went on, "and as you are aware, your father's yacht is waiting for you in Miami."

Orina clasped her hands together.

"You are saying something that I have wanted to do for a long time—to get away and have a chance to think about myself and my future."

She knew as she spoke that she was really

escaping from the men who had pursued her in London.

In New York she thought they were like a pack of wolves ready to devour her at any moment.

"You can go anywhere you like," Bernard Hoffman was saying, "but I suggest that a trip to the Gulf of Mexico would be interesting."

"Yes, yes, of course," Orina agreed.

She was not particularly interested in her destination.

All she wanted to do was to get away.

She wanted to forget that ghastly moment when she had seen Clint Hunter lying on the floor and had thought he was dead.

"You will have to take Mrs. Carswright with you," Bernard Hoffman was saying.

Orina gave a little cry.

"Oh, must I? I would far rather be alone."

He smiled.

"I think it would be difficult for anyone to believe that you were, and it would certainly give the gossips something about which to speculate unceasingly."

Orina shrugged her shoulders.

"Very well then, Mrs. Carswright, but I refuse to have yet another woman on board. Papa always said that women servants at sea were a nuisance because they were always sea-sick."

"I remember him saying that, not once, but a dozen times!" Bernard Hoffman said. "In which case, you need take no one else, and, as you know, there is a steward aboard who, as your father often said, was the best valet and nursemaid he had ever known!"

Orina gave a shaky little laugh.

"I know that James will look after me, but what I really want to do is to look after myself and be alone."

"I will make all the arrangements for you to leave to-morrow morning," Bernard Hoffman said. "In the meantime write a charming and sympathetic note to that young fool Hunter and I will see that an enormous arrangement of flowers is sent to the Hospital."

"What . . . what shall I do if he dies?" Orina asked in a low voice.

"He is a healthy young man, and I see no reason why he should," Bernard Hoffman replied. "He will doubtless be in Hospital for a long time and the accident will not have improved his health in the future—but that is his business!"

He frowned before he added:

"I have no use for weak young men who behave in this melodramatic manner over women, even if they are as pretty as you!"

"I hate all men!" Orina said suddenly. "I hate them! I hate them and you had better be prepared for me never to marry but to spend the rest of my life running Papa's various business interests."

She paused before she went on:

"At least machinery cannot make a nuisance of itself!"

Bernard Hoffman laughed.

"On the contrary, it causes a great deal of trouble, sometimes to those who have to look after it, and to owners like yourself who can lose money if it does not give so brilliant a performance as is expected of it."

Orina was not really listening.

She was thinking of the letters she had received that morning from two of her English suitors who were coming to New York.

She was expecting them within the next few weeks.

She went to her writing-desk and picked up the letters that were lying on it.

"These are from Lord Airsdale and Sir Montagu Seymour," she said. "When they arrive, I am sure they will make every effort to follow me wherever I am, so tell them I have gone to Newfoundland."

"That is not a bad suggestion," Bernard Hoffman said slowly. "It would be a difficult place to contact you, so that is where I shall tell the Press you have gone."

"Thank you . . . thank you!" Orina replied. "And please apologise for me to all those people who are expecting me to attend their Balls, Receptions, and Heaven knows what else in the next three weeks."

"They will be very disappointed to find that their 'Star' is not in evidence," Bernard Hoffman said. "But I am sure you are doing the right thing, and there is no need for you to return until you are bored."

"I warn you that may be never!" Orina replied.

She knew as she spoke that he smiled a little cynically.

She could read his thoughts.

He was thinking that, having been such an overwhelming success both in London and New York, she would soon find the solitude of her own company somewhat unstimulating.

"When you do come back," he said aloud, "I suggest that if Hunter is still being tiresome, you pay a visit to your grandfather. You know he would be delighted to see you."

"And I would like to see Grandpapa," Orina said. "It is not he who makes me reluctant to go to England, but the men who will be waiting there, proposing, begging, grabbing at me as if I was a golden carp!"

Bernard Hoffman threw back his head and laughed.

"You may laugh," Orina said bitterly, "but you have no idea what it is like to feel that you might be harpooned at any moment, or in some treacherous manner enticed into a cage from which you cannot escape!"

"Is it really as bad as that?" Bernard Hoffman asked.

"It is worse . . . much worse," she replied, "and as you well know, it is not me they want, but my money!"

Bernard Hoffman smiled again.

"Now you are being ultra-modest. I think a great many men want you for yourself, and, because I know the English quite well, a great number of the men there will not approach you *because* you are so rich. An Englishman likes to be master of his own Castle!"

Orina was silent before she said:

"Englishmen are also snobby, stuck-up, auto-cratic, and look disdainfully at any other nation. They think their women are not good enough for them."

There was a note in her voice that Bernard Hoffman did not miss.

Then, as if he thought this conversation was only adding to her distress, he said:

"I am now going to put the wheels in motion which will carry you in comfort to Miami to-morrow, and all you have to do is to tell your maid what clothes you intend to take with you. And do not forget a bathing-dress."

Orina laughed because it was not what she expected him to say.

"As I intend to be away for a long time," she said, "I will also take my fur-lined boots!"

Bernard Hoffman would have left the room, but she put her hand on his arm.

"You know I am grateful," she said, "and now that Papa is no longer here, I rely on you for everything. I know you will not fail me."

"I admired your father more than any other man I have ever met," Bernard Hoffman replied. "He was the kindest and the best friend any man could have. I would therefore never fail either him, or you."

"Thank you," Orina said.

As she went from the room, Bernard Hoffman looked after her with a worried expression in his eyes.

He knew there was something wrong ever since she had returned from England.

He had not tried to gain her confidence, feeling that sooner or later he would learn what troubled her.

No one, however, was more aware than he was that the behaviour of young Hunter could do her an immeasurable amount of harm.

He could only pray that his explanation of what had occurred would be believed.

But the New Yorkers always enjoyed a drama.

They would doubtless at this very moment be exaggerating it and trying to make it as lurid and dramatic as possible.

"Goddamn the young fool!" he said to himself. "Why the hell can he not control his emotions rather than try to mess up the life of a girl who is far too good for him in every way?"

Bernard Hoffman had loved Orina ever since she was a child.

As he had gone almost everywhere with Dale Vandeholt, he had seen a great deal of her.

He had watched her grow from an adorable toddler into an attractive little ten-year-old.

She might have stepped straight out of a Picture-Book.

She was arrestingly beautiful, even at that age.

Dale Vandeholt had often discussed with Bernard Hoffman what would happen to her in the future.

"You know as well as I do, Bernard," he had said once, "that having a great deal of money, for a woman, is a mistake. She will be pursued by fortune-hunters and she will find it very difficult to know when a man loves her with his heart and soul and not just with greedy eyes."

"If Orina has your perception, Dale," Bernard Hoffman had replied, "she will have some idea of whether a man is genuine or not."

"I hope you are right," Dale Vandeholt replied, "but I am worried—extremely worried!"

There was silence until Bernard Hoffman said a little hesitatingly:

"You know, Dale, the solution is quite easy. You could marry again, and you might have a son—or several of them for that matter!"

Dale Vandeholt smiled.

"I have thought of it—of course I have—but I was so ideally happy with my wife that I am desperately afraid not only to risk spoiling my own future, but also damaging the memory of something that was utterly and completely perfect."

Bernard Hoffman understood.

Dale Vandeholt was a very attractive man.

Apart from his money, a great many American women were looking at him speculatively.

It was obvious they would be ready to fall into his arms if he ever approached them.

But Dale had died without remarrying and Orina had inherited all his great possessions.

"She is too young for such responsibility," Bernard Hoffman told himself as he had done so often before.

There was nothing he could do about it except try to protect her as best he could.

Where he could not help her was with the depression that swept over her as she entered her father's Private Drawing-Room in his Railroad Car.

It had been attached to the train which would carry her to Miami.

Her father possessed one on practically every line that left from New York.

She had travelled with him in them so often.

As the train moved out of the station, she felt as if he were sitting beside her and guiding her.

Mrs. Carswright had been helped into a seat that was not over the wheels.

A rug was placed over her knees.

She was an elderly woman whom her father had chosen to live in the house as Orina's Chaperone after her mother had died.

He had deliberately chosen somebody older because he thought she would not interfere too much in Orina's life.

She would also not be jealous or in any way try to compete with his daughter.

Mrs. Carswright's antecedents were impeccable.

She was born in one of the most respected Southern families and was the widow of the Bishop of New York.

She was a pleasant, gentle person.

At the same time, Orina had discovered as soon as they met that she was also a bore.

She never had anything original to say, but was always pleasant to everybody she met.

The Dowagers of New York accepted her as one of themselves.

That was all Dale Vandeholt had wanted.

Mrs. Carswright had become part of the furniture in their huge house on Fifth Avenue.

Although Orina was always polite to her, most of the time she forgot her very existence.

Mrs. Carswright had not been particularly perturbed at having to leave at a moment's notice.

She had long ago ceased to be surprised at anything the Vandeholts did.

Moving from one place to another with very little notice was one of them.

She merely allowed her maid to pack her clothes as Orina's maid was packing hers.

The next morning they were in a comfortable carriage and on their way to the station.

Bernard Hoffman, of course, saw them off.

"If there is anything you want," he said to Orina, "telegraph me and I will see that you get it as soon as possible."

"I will do that," Orina answered, "but please, write to me and tell me what is happening. Do not be surprised, however, if you receive very few letters."

"You get more like your father every day," Bernard Hoffman said. "He always disliked letter-writing, and would dictate instructions through a Secretary to convey his orders as swiftly as possible."

"I am afraid you will not even have that," Orina said, "but thank you once again for looking after me, as you always have done."

"Take good care of yourself," Bernard Hoffman said, "and as I am sure you know, Captain Bennett is a sensible man, so ask his advice before you do anything rash."

Orina laughed.

"I am going to think about myself," she said. "I enjoy being alone which, if you think about it, is something that has not happened for years."

"It should be interesting for you to get to know a young lady called Orina Vandeholt," Bernard Hoffman said, "and you may find she surprises even you!"

"That is what interests me," Orina answered, and they both laughed.

The train moved off, and Orina waved until Bernard Hoffman was out of sight.

"He is the kindest man I have ever met," she told herself, "and I am not surprised Papa trusted him."

She knew he had the reputation of being very ruthless where business was concerned.

That was something she understood and realised was sometimes necessary.

It was that determination, which could be called ruthlessness, which had made her father so outstanding.

It was something, she thought, that was lamentably lacking in the young men she met.

They seemed to drift through life, interested only in amusing themselves.

She sat down in a seat that was at the other end of the Drawing-Room from Mrs. Carswright.

She thought that where Englishmen were concerned, they expended their brains on sport more than on anything else.

Her grandfather had told her laughingly that most Englishmen were more devoted to their dogs than to their children.

Where their wives were concerned, he added, horses came first.

She knew he was teasing her.

At the same time, when she had made her debut and met a great number of Englishmen, she thought there was a lot of truth in what he said.

She was quite certain, if she married one, how her money would be spent.

It would be on breeding a horse that would win the Derby and the Gold Cup at Ascot.

Her husband's fox-hounds would undoubtedly be the finest pack in the whole of Britain.

Americans were different.

She had met men who were absorbedly interested in their businesses, but only so that they could make money.

With them, it was money that counted and not Industry itself, not the fact that they were contributing to the progress of the United States.

That was where her father had been so different.

She knew that he had really cared.

He was building up American products, which in the future would make it the most powerful Nation in the world.

"We have a long way to go," he had said, "because we are a new country. We have great facilities, great natural resources which are not yet properly exploited, but what we most need, my Darling, is brains."

"That is what you have, Papa," Orina said.

"I like to think so," he answered. "But I am one man and this country is very large. We need young men who really care, who want to carry the 'Stars and Stripes' to every corner of the world as the British have done with the 'Union Jack.' "

Orina knew he was thinking of the maps she had studied when she was in England.

Half the world was the British Empire, coloured in red.

"What you ought to be, Papa, is President," she said. "Then I am sure you could inspire many more people to think as you do."

Her father had, however, held up his hands in horror.

"That is the last thing I want," he exclaimed. "I am a 'doer,' not a talker, and it is the 'doers' of America who are going to make it great."

As the train gathered speed, Orina was saying as she had said a thousand times before:

"How could Papa have died when he was so needed, when there is so much to be done and so few people capable of doing it?"

She knew she was being unjust.

At the same time, the men she met, the men with whom she danced and who asked her to marry them, had all been inferior both in character and personality to her father.

"I shall never marry," she told herself as she had already told Bernard Hoffman.

'Instead,' she went on in her mind, 'I shall enlarge and increase Papa's Empire so that if he were alive, he would be as proud of me as if I had been a son.'

She was well aware that it was going to be difficult to achieve anything so great because she was a woman.

American women might be the boss in their homes and nag their husbands in private.

But where business was concerned, nobody listened to anything they had to say.

The doors of an Office and a Boardroom were closed against them.

"Perhaps with Bernard's help I will be able to change all that," Orina told herself.

Then she wondered if that was what she really wanted.

The trouble was she did not know what she required of life.

But somehow it was not the superficial endless search for amusement which she had found both in London and in New York.

The train travelled on.

She sat thinking quietly about her future until it was time to move into her Sleeping-Compartment and go to bed.

*　　*　　*

The sunshine when they reached Miami made it look beautiful.

Everything had been arranged for her as Orina might have expected.

There were carriages to meet her at the station.

One took her to the harbour, where her father's yacht was waiting.

It had recently been in dry dock for an overhaul, also to have added to it some new ideas that Dale Vandeholt had ordered just before he died.

It was, Orina knew, the largest, finest, and most magnificent private ship afloat.

Captain Bennett was ready to greet her as she stepped up the gangway.

Nothing, she thought, could have looked more spick and span than the seamen who were carrying aboard her luggage.

Two junior officers were helping Mrs. Carswright.

She thanked them in her soft Southern voice for their kindness.

"It is great to see you, Miss Orina!" Captain Bennett said.

"I am delighted to come aboard, Captain," Orina answered.

"Of course, the first question," he said as he smiled, "is—where do you wish to go?!"

"From one end of the world to the other!" Orina replied. "But Mr. Hoffman suggested we might first explore the Gulf of Mexico."

"That is just what I was thinking myself," the Captain said. "The weather is right for it, and it is an area I do not remember you and your father visiting. I am sure there will be a great deal there to interest you."

"That is what I thought," Orina answered, "and as there is no hurry, Captain, we can stop wherever there is a Pyramid or something exciting to see."

"I think you will find that most of those are inland," the Captain said, "at the same time, there are small bays and beaches which I am sure you will enjoy. You have only to tell me what you require and I will do my best to provide it."

"Thank you," Orina said, "and of course I want

to see all the new gadgets you have on the yacht."

"Then it will surprise you," the Captain said, "and only your father could have thought of anything so different from any other ship afloat!"

Finally they started to leave harbour.

Orina thought no one would believe that she was travelling on this very large vessel entirely on her own, except, of course, for an elderly lady.

She could imagine that most of her contemporaries would have wanted to take a young man with them.

They could then have someone with whom to dance, talk, and flirt.

Now, as she went to her cabin, which was very beautiful, she was thinking how lucky she was to be alone.

The Captain had asked her if she wanted to use her father's Stateroom.

It was the Master Cabin and the largest.

But Orina had preferred the one she always used.

It had been specially decorated for her and had been hers ever since the yacht was first built.

Her father had had another yacht when her mother had been alive.

It was very comfortable and decorated beautifully to her taste.

They had spent many voyages alone on it and it was to him sacred because they had been so happy.

After her death Dale Vandeholt had set out to build another yacht which was larger and more magnificent, not particularly a boat for love, which was what the first one had been.

Orina had understood.

When he had come aboard with her he had not been haunted by the ghost of her mother waiting for him with outstretched arms.

Now, as she thought of it, she supposed some of her reluctance to marry any man stemmed from those years.

She was comparing the love they offered her with that of her father and mother.

It was something of which she had been aware from the moment she had been born.

They were so deeply and overwhelmingly in love that it was difficult to think of them apart.

After her mother had died she had gradually understood that her father was not complete in himself.

It was something that was very difficult to put into words.

Yet, she knew that was what she wanted in her life.

What was more, she was not prepared to settle for second best.

In the darkness of her cabin Orina asked herself how she could possibly marry a man like Clint Hunter?

She tried not to think of him.

But it was inevitable that she should feel guilty.

At the same time, she wondered how could she help refusing a man who was stupid enough to try to take his own life?

'If he behaves like that, there might be other men who would do the same,' she argued.

It was a frightening thought.

But it was one she knew would haunt her every time a man asked her to become his wife.

*   *   *

When Bernard Hoffman had seen her off at the station, he had told her he had already enquired about Clint Hunter at the Hospital.

"He passed a restful night," he told Orina, "and I think the Surgeons are confident that he will survive, although it will naturally take time before his wound heals."

There was a slight note of contempt in Bernard Hoffman's voice which Orina did not miss.

She had thought that it was impossible to respect a man who would do anything so hurtful, not only to himself, but also to the woman he professed to love.

"Of course I do not hate Clint," she told herself in the darkness, "but I do despise him as I despise any man who cannot stand up to adversity as Papa would have done."

She then remembered that she was starting out on a Voyage of Discovery.

It was not going to be easy to make decisions about the future, but that was what she had to do.

Everything at the moment seemed to hurt her.

She knew sensibly that she was, in fact, suffering from shock after what had occurred.

'I will relax, enjoy the sunshine, and think about Papa,' she decided.

It would be an agony to know that he was not

in the next cabin, that she could not run to him and tell him what she was feeling.

She was somewhat uncertain as to what she believed about death.

Was there another world with which one could communicate, as some people believed?

If so, could she reach out to it?

Would her father be there, waiting to help her?

On the other hand, was there nothing?

It seemed a terrible waste of a person's brain.

If, after all her father had achieved, after all he had worked at and inaugurated, he was just an empty body lying in the Churchyard?

Everything within her rebelled against the wastefulness of anything like that.

Yet the majority of people thought, unless they were religious, that death was the end.

"What does it matter," one of the girls at School had asked, "if, when we die, we go to Heaven and sit round a sapphire sea, twanging a harp. I cannot see that helps me at the moment!"

Orina agreed with her. It was certainly something she did not wish to do herself.

On the other hand, one of the girls who was more intelligent than the others said:

"All religions since the very beginning say that Death is not the end, and the majority of Eastern religions believe we come back in another body."

"How does that help us?" a girl asked. "If I am in another body now, I cannot see that I would feel any happier if I had been a Roman in the past, or perhaps a native in some African desert."

Orina had laughed at this.

At the same time, she had understood the question.

"Perhaps on this voyage I shall find the answer not only to Life, but to Death," she told herself.

Then, for the first time since the horror of Clint Hunter shooting himself, she felt the tears come into her eyes.

She was crying not for him, but for herself.

She was crying because she was living in a world which no longer contained her father.

He had been so different from any other man she had ever met.

"Papa! Papa!" she called in the darkness. "How can you have left me? Why can I not reach you wherever you are? Surely you mind that I am alone and understand I need your help?"

She spoke aloud without really meaning to.

Now, as her voice died away, she was aware of nothing but silence except for the lap of the water on the sides of the yacht.

chapter three

FOR the next two days they steamed slowly and comfortably through the Gulf of Mexico.

The weather, however, grew rough, and the Captain set course for the shore.

They stopped for the night at small unknown bays.

Using his own initiative, Captain Bennett moved on the next morning before breakfast.

Mrs. Carswright had appeared at mealtimes.

Otherwise she either rested in her cabin or else was helped onto a long chair on deck which supported her feet.

When they had luncheon together yesterday, she had very little to say.

After a long silence at dinner, which was early, Orina asked:

"Are you quite well? I had not noticed before,

but you do look a little pale."

"I am quite all right, my dear," Mrs. Carswright said. "I have just been having some strange pains lately, but I dislike doctors and hate having them fussing over me."

"That is what Papa always said," Orina replied, "but if you are in pain, I think you should see a good Specialist."

"I have some pills that help me to sleep and take the pain away," Mrs. Carswright replied, "and I really need nothing else."

She spoke so positively that Orina thought it would be a mistake to interfere.

At the same time, she hoped she was not going to be ill.

She knew how much her father had disliked ill people aboard the yacht.

It was why he had always insisted that Orina should look after herself and not have a Lady's-Maid with her.

Mrs. Carswright was different.

Orina remembered a little belatedly that she was growing old.

'She must certainly be careful not to fall or trip up if the weather is rough,' she thought.

On the third morning she realised the sea was somewhat tempestuous.

She was not surprised to find herself having breakfast alone.

"Is Mrs. Carswright all right?" she asked the steward.

"Ah've taken her breakfast to her cabin, Miss," the steward replied, "but she says she's not hungry, and I think the reason is she'm feelin' sea-sick."

Orina groaned.

Her father was right.

If Mrs. Carswright was very sick, they would have to put into port until the sea was calmer.

Orina enjoyed the battle of the waves breaking over the bow.

She had never been sick whatever the weather was like.

When she had finished her breakfast, she went up on the Bridge to be with the Captain.

"I am afraid Mrs. Carswright is not well," she said, "and if it becomes any rougher, I do think we shall have to put into port in case it upsets her."

"We will do that," Captain Bennett replied. "At the same time, I am rather eager to try out this new engine your father installed and see how it copes in a really rough sea."

Orina smiled.

"There is nothing Papa would have enjoyed more, but I feel it will not be rough enough here and we should wait and see how the weather is in the Atlantic."

"That is what I would enjoy," Captain Bennett agreed, "providing there are no squeamish people aboard."

Orina stayed on the Bridge until it was nearly time for luncheon.

Then she thought she should visit Mrs. Carswright.

She went below only to learn from the Steward,

who was looking after her, that she was asleep.

"Now, don' you fret, Miss Orina," he said. "Ah's takin' good care of the lady, and the more she sleeps, the better."

Orina looked at him suspiciously.

"Have you given her a sleeping-draught?" she asked.

"Weren't no need, Ma'am. She's taking some herself to stop the pain from which she's suffering."

'I should not have taken her with me,' Orina thought.

But everything had happened so hastily that she had left everything to Bernard Hoffman.

She felt certain he would not have allowed her to go without a Chaperone.

The sea abated a little towards the afternoon.

When once again Orina tried to see Mrs. Carswright, she was told that she was still asleep.

Orina, therefore, spent her time on deck and enjoyed being with the Captain.

Once again her father had been right in choosing an engine which did not even have to slow down however tempestuous the sea might be.

She was not able to see Mrs. Carswright before she went to bed.

She thought, however, she would sleep peacefully, because they had anchored where there was a cliff protecting them.

The movement of the yacht was therefore very slight.

When she was awoken in the morning James

came into the cabin to pull back the curtains over the port-hole.

When he saw that she was awake he said quietly:

"Ah's got some bad news for you, Miss Orina, and don' y'all take it too much to heart."

"What has happened?" Orina asked.

"Th' old lady passed away in her sleep."

"I do not believe it!" Orina exclaimed.

"She didn't suffer none, an' there were a smile on her face like she knowed the Gates of Heaven was opened for her," James said.

When he had gone, Orina jumped out of bed.

She put on her dressing-gown and went to Mrs. Carswright's cabin.

James had already crossed her hands over her breast, and she thought he had also smoothed her hair.

She looked younger than she had when she had been alive.

As James had said, there was a smile on her lips and she seemed at peace.

Orina stood looking at her for some time.

Then she went down on her knees and prayed.

She went back to her own cabin feeling guilty.

She should, however, have enquired before bringing Mrs. Carswright aboard whether the voyage would prove too much for her.

Then Orina told herself sensibly that if she had to die, she would perhaps have rather died without all the commotion of doctors and nurses.

Also without relations hovering over her and questioning as to whether she had made a Will.

'It is the way I would like to die myself,' she thought.

At the same time, she still felt vaguely responsible.

The Captain, however, was a "tower of strength."

"You are not to blame yourself, Miss Orina," he said. "The only mistake was that Mrs. Carswright should have told you she was in pain before she came aboard."

"Will we have to go back?" Orina asked a little nervously.

There might be newspaper interest in Mrs. Carswright's death because she had been the wife of the Bishop of New York.

If so, there could be questions as to why she was accompanying a young girl in an otherwise empty yacht in the height of the Social Season.

Orina drew in her breath.

She felt sure the newspapers would somehow manage to connect it with Clint Hunter's "accident" with the revolver.

Almost as if the Captain read her thoughts, he said:

"As Mr. Hoffman was so insistent on you taking a long trip, Miss Orina, I'm thinking it would be wisest if we buried Mrs. Carswright at sea."

Orina looked at him in surprise.

"Can you do that?" she asked after a moment.

"Of course I can," the Captain replied. "As Captain of this ship I'm empowered to bury or marry any of my passengers should it be required, and I'm quite sure Mrs. Carswright'll not be missed until we return to New York."

Orina knew this would be the best thing possible as far as she was concerned.

At the same time, she could not help feeling it a pity that there would be so few mourners for poor Mrs. Carswright.

The Captain took the yacht way out to sea and out of sight of land.

By this time the waves had subsided, and the sun enveloped everything in a golden haze.

Mrs. Carswright had been wrapped in white sheets, and her body, stitched in canvas, was covered with the Stars and Stripes.

The Captain then performed the Funeral Service very movingly.

Then the body slid slowly into the water. The seamen saluted respectfully.

It was a very dignified, simple Service.

Orina thought it was the way she would like to be buried rather than have all the pomp and ceremony that had accompanied her father's Funeral.

It had taken place in the small Church that was only about a mile from the Ranch.

His ornate coffin had been carried there on a wagon that was pulled by six of his finest horses.

The coffin was covered with flowers.

Behind it walked first Orina, then Bernard Hoffman and a number of her father's Secretaries and Managers.

After them had come all the people from the Estate.

One of them was leading his favourite horse with

her father's black riding-boots in reverse attached to the saddle.

The Church itself, on Orina's instructions, was massed with flowers.

It was packed to suffocation with people who had come from every part of America as well as from New York.

Not everyone had been able to be seated inside it.

There was also a huge crowd outside, listening through the open doors to the Service and the hymns which were beautifully sung.

It had been a very impressive, grand Funeral for a very important man.

Orina had thought that she could almost hear her father laughing at the pomposity of it all.

Mrs. Carswright's body disappeared beneath the waves.

Orina knew that, if he had the choice, this was the way her father would have preferred to be buried.

When the Service was over, the engines started up once again and Orina went below.

Because she felt it was somehow more respectful, she stayed in her cabin rather than going up on deck.

She lay on her bed and tried to pray for Mrs. Carswright.

She thought it was sad that, try as she would, it was impossible to pretend that she would miss her.

She had been such a very nebulous person, someone who had never said anything she could remember.

Her life had seemed as monotonous and boring as she had been herself.

"I ought to have cared more," Orina told herself.

But she found it was impossible to think of other things rather than the woman who had just been buried at sea.

* * *

They sailed back towards the land and were now far down in the South of the Gulf.

It was far hotter, Orina knew, than if they had been in the North.

She had the idea that this part of Mexico was more primitive and less inhabited than any other part.

She really knew very little about it.

She wished she had had time to study some books on Mexico before they had left New York.

Thinking back, she could not remember her father ever talking about it.

He had once said that, when he had the time, he would like to visit Mexico City, and see some of the Pyramids and tombs that had recently been discovered.

One thing Orina did remember was that Spanish was the language of Mexico.

She could remember being taught at School about the invasion of Mexico by the Spaniards in 1500.

It was not until this century that they had been driven away, when the country had become a Republic.

"That is enough to be going on with," she told herself laughingly, "and I will find out more when I see the country itself."

They entered what she realised was a small Port late that evening.

She learnt it was called Sadaro but it did not seem very impressive.

"I hope the natives are friendly," Captain Bennett said, "if not, we'll have to move on."

"Friendly?" Orina asked in surprise. "Why should they be anything else?"

"In some parts of Mexico they still resent strangers, and tourists are not welcome," he replied.

"Good gracious, I had no idea of that!" Orina exclaimed. "I thought Americans were welcomed everywhere, especially where the people are poor."

There was a slightly sarcastic note in her voice, but the Captain replied seriously:

"Money is not always as welcome as we like to think it is and, as I say, I'll make enquiries as to what sort of place it is before you, Miss Orina, go ashore."

Orina was quite certain that he was fussing unnecessarily.

She was, therefore, not surprised the next morning when James told her:

"Capt'n Bennett say everyone wishin' to come aboard, ready to sell us the shirts off their backs and the shoes off their feet!"

"The 'Almighty Dollar' wins again!" she said. "But I am glad, because I want to explore."

"You's not going alone, Miss Orina?" James asked.

"Of course I am!" Orina replied. "And you know as well as I do that if Mrs. Carswright had been alive, she would not have come with me. She would have found it too hot and undoubtedly the ground would have been too hard for her to walk on."

"Then don' y'all go too far," James said. "You never can tell with them foreigners, Miss Orina!"

Orina laughed.

She fetched a sunshade from her cabin.

Then she went down the gangway onto the grubby Quay that needed repairing.

It was obvious at first sight that Sadaro was very poor.

The houses were all in need of paint.

The windows were cracked and the people who stared at her when she appeared were poorly dressed.

She walked on.

She moved from the water's edge into what she found was actually bigger than a *hacienda*. It was almost a small town.

What was strange after the poverty of the houses she had seen so far was to find a large and prosperous building looking dazzlingly white in the sunshine.

She stopped at a shop where there was a display of fruit and vegetables.

She asked the owner in Spanish who it was who lived in the big house.

"It's Government House, *Señorita*," he replied.

He did not say any more.

Orina wanted to ask why the Governor should be so comfortable while the people around him were clearly in need of assistance.

This was very obvious when she saw the children.

Barefooted and in rags, some of them were wearing nothing but a tattered shirt.

They were very attractive.

The Indians had large eyes and looked at her pleadingly.

They were, she thought, begging, like small puppies, for something to eat.

She bought some fruit and gave some avocados and bananas to three small children.

They were staring at her as if she were a being from another Planet.

Instantly, as if they had sprung out of the very ground, there was a crowd of them.

Yet they were far better behaved, she thought, than the children in the slums of New York, or of London.

They did not beg or hold out their hands.

They merely stood looking at her.

It was impossible not to give each one of them some of the fruit.

The Shopkeeper was delighted.

When she paid him what seemed to her a very small sum for a considerable amount of fruit, he bowed respectfully.

It was then that an older child, a little better dressed, came up to her.

She had a piece of paper and a pencil in her hands.

"Please, *Señorita*," she pleaded in Spanish, "write for me your name."

This had often happened to Orina in New York, and she smiled.

She took the piece of paper from the girl and set it on the table which contained the fruit.

"Please, *Señorita*, graciously write my names!"

"What are they?" Orina enquired.

"Maria-Theresa Arabella Lopez."

Orina laughed.

"A big, big name for a small person!" she exclaimed.

But she wrote the names down and added her own.

"Thank you, thank you, *Señorita*," the girl cried, and curtsied.

Orina would have walked farther, but as soon as she moved from the shop the children followed her.

Now she told them in her best Spanish that there would be no more fruit, but they would not leave her.

Finally, telling herself it was her own fault for feeding them, she returned to the yacht.

"It is an extraordinary place," she told the Captain, who had been waiting eagerly for her return.

"In what way?" he asked.

"Well, there is the most impressive Government House," Orina said, "on which a considerable amount of money has obviously been spent, but the houses in the village are all dilapidated and, as far as I could see, all the inhabitants are in rags!"

"That is not hard to believe," Captain Bennett said. "Governments are often corrupt and a bad

Governor will look after himself and not worry about his people."

"Then they should be fired!" Orina said hotly. "And the children, besides being in rags, were very thin."

"I'm afraid you will find that in a great number of places in Mexico," the Captain replied. "The Mexicans are very efficient in some ways, but uncivilised in others. And while the businessmen and prospectors flourish, the Indians are persecuted and enslaved as they were from the beginning of the conquest until the very end of it."

"I am sure it would have upset Papa if he had come here," Orina said. "He loathed cruelty, and I remember now reading at School how cruel the conquering Spaniards were."

"That is true," Captain Bennett agreed. "I remember when I first came here some years ago hearing how badly the Indians were treated. Yet somehow a great number of them managed to survive."

*　*　*

After luncheon Orina sat on the shady side of the deck under an awning.

It had been erected as soon as they entered the Port.

She lifted up her feet and opened a book.

She had found it on the shelves which her father had put up in the Saloon.

She had noticed it just before luncheon was served and saw with delight it was about Mexico.

This was what she had been longing to find.

She had read only two or three pages when a steward approached her.

"What is it?" she enquired.

"There's a man here, Miss Orina, who wishes to speak with you."

"What about?" Orina asked.

"He told me to say, Miss, that he urgently requires your help."

"By which I guess he is going to ask me for money."

She remembered what had happened in the morning.

Give a piece of fruit to a child and in an instant there are several dozen of them.

"Tell the man I am resting," she said, "and, if he persists, tell him I am not staying long in Sadaro. I therefore cannot concern myself in local affairs."

The Steward grinned.

"I guess that's wise, Miss!" he said. "One beggar always leads to another!"

"That is true," Orina agreed. "Anyhow, get rid of him."

The Steward disappeared and she returned to her book.

It was very interesting and all about the ancient history of Mexico.

She read for the rest of the afternoon.

It had grown cooler, then, and a Steward brought her a drink of lime-juice, which she preferred to tea.

As he put it down beside her, he said:

"Ah doesn't know if you'd be interested, Miss,

but there's some men here wanting to show you their horses."

Orina looked up in surprise.

Then she said:

"I have just been reading in this book that at one time after the Spaniards had conquered the country the Indians were not allowed to mount horses."

"That must have been a li'l hard on them when there was no other way of getting about, 'cept on your bare feet!"

"That is true," Orina replied.

She did not tell him, but the book told her that the horses had soon grown wild and had to be tamed.

Because horses became important both economically and culturally, a new breed of men had developed.

On the ranches they had become outstanding horsemen through sheer necessity.

This information, even though it applied to the past, made her think that the horses might be worth looking at.

Perhaps Mexico would have horses that could be added to the large Stud her father had built up on his Ranch.

She jumped up, and putting down her book, followed the Steward to the other side of the yacht.

On the Quay there were four horses.

They were ridden by young men who, to her surprise, were better dressed than she had expected.

She went down the gangway.

When she saw the horses she realised in fact

that they were well worth looking at.

They were, in fact, different from any she had seen previously.

The young men in charge of them spoke Spanish.

It was a little more traditional than the Spanish spoken by the Shopkeeper and the children.

She therefore managed to converse with them quite fluently.

They asked her if she would like to ride one of their horses.

"I would like that very much," she said as she smiled.

"Now—or to-morrow?" one of the young men asked.

Orina thought for a minute, and they remained silent until she replied.

"I would like to go out from the village into the interior of the country."

She made a gesture with her hand which they obviously understood.

"We take you, *Señorita*, on our best horses. What time?"

She told them nine o'clock and they promised to call back for her then.

With a little piece of mime, because the right words escaped her, she explained that she did not want to ride side-saddle, but astride.

She thought they understood.

Saluting her, obviously delighted that she would ride with them, they rode away.

Captain Bennett was waiting for her on deck.

"I hope those horses can carry you safely," he remarked.

"They seemed well-bred to me," Orina replied, "and you know I am a very experienced rider."

"I am not thinking of that," Captain Bennett said, "but as far as I can ascertain, there is nothing historical about this part of the country, so you need not travel too far."

"I have suggested to the young men that I would like to see the country beyond the town," Orina replied, "and quite frankly, Captain, I shall enjoy the exercise."

Captain Bennett was amused.

"I thought you would soon tire of the inactivity of sitting about like a 'Lady of leisure.' You are like your father. If he was quiet for one day, he behaved as if he had taken three months' holiday."

"That is true," Orina replied. "But I wish he could have been here. I know he would be interested in seeing this country, which I feel contains a great many mysteries."

"If your father was with us, I am quite certain he would unearth a Pyramid or some treasure that has never been discovered before," the Captain said. "He had a presentiment about things which is not given to ordinary people like us."

"That is true," Orina said sadly, "he always knew what was wanted, then was determined to supply it."

The Captain laughed before he said:

"I miss him, Miss Orina, I miss him a great deal!"

He walked away before Orina could reply.

She knew it was because he did not wish her to

know how emotional he felt.

"How could Papa have died so soon?" she asked, looking up at the sky.

There was no answer, and she felt suddenly defiant and angry with the whole world.

"Why should there be tragedies, and why should someone so wanted and who was doing so much to improve America be struck down in that cruel manner?"

She wanted to rail at Fate; she wanted to punish someone for what was an unnecessary disaster, not only to herself, but also to thousands of people whom her father had hunted and employed.

"It is unfair!" she stormed to herself. "Wrong and unfair, but there is nothing I can do about it. I hate a world where there appears to be no justice!"

She felt as she spoke as if she were challenging God Himself because He had allowed this to happen, just for the senselessness that there had been frost in the air and ice underfoot.

She no longer wanted to cry over her father's death, but in some way to avenge it.

But how she could do so she had no idea.

She knew only that as soon as he had died, everything had seemed to go wrong.

She was alone, pressured by men like Clint Hunter, threatened with a scandal which her father would have dealt with.

Now, like a ship without a rudder tossing in a stormy sea, she had no idea where she was going or why.

She only knew that she disliked the world in which she lived.

In the same way, she disliked the men who lived in it.

She picked up her book on Mexico, but she no longer wished to read about the past.

The Spaniards had come and gone; the people had been tortured and massacred.

The merciful God in whom they had believed had not saved them.

What was the answer?

In what could she believe or not believe?

When she went to bed, she lay awake for a long time staring into the darkness.

She knew that for the first time in her life she had found a great deal to hate.

But nothing at all to love.

chapter four

ORINA had her breakfast early in her cabin.

She then dressed herself in the clothes she wore when she was riding on her father's Ranch.

Strangely enough, it was called "a Mexican habit" and she had always expected to see them when she went to that country.

The divided skirt was bright green, fringed down either side and round the hem.

It fitted snugly into her waist and, when she put on her boots, made her look very dashing.

There was a jacket as well, but it was far too hot to need it.

She therefore wore a silk blouse which was the same colour and which, sensibly, had long sleeves.

She knew that, if the sun was very hot, it was a mistake for any part of the body to be exposed.

It could become red and blistered unless one was careful.

Her mother had always insisted, when they were on the Ranch, that she wear a large-brimmed hat. Again, Mexican fashion, Orina's was tied under her chin.

When she was dressed she thought perhaps she looked too smart after what she had seen of the inhabitants of Sadaro.

There had been few people about when she had walked in the town, with the exception of the children.

She therefore decided she was sure she was unlikely to have an audience.

When she went up on deck just after nine o'clock, the Captain was waiting for her.

"I hear, Miss Orina, that you intend to go riding."

"Yes," Orina answered. "The horses they showed me yesterday were, to my surprise, quite outstanding for this part of the world."

The Captain looked worried.

"I hope they are properly broken in," he said. "I would not like you to have an accident."

Orina knew he was thinking of her, and she said quickly:

"As you know, Captain, I have ridden since I was a baby and I doubt if there is any horse in Mexico or anywhere else in the world I could not control."

She thought as she spoke that it sounded boastful, but the worry went from the Captain's eyes.

"I hope you will be all right," he said. "I wish

I could send somebody with you, but on this yacht my men are all sailors and not so good on land."

Orina laughed.

" 'Each man to his trade!' " she quoted. "I promise you I will be all right."

She ran down the gangway to where the horses were waiting.

There were two of the young men she had spoken to the day before.

There was a third horse which was even finer than those she had inspected before.

She patted it, and inspected the girths to ensure that they were tight enough.

Then, as one of the men knelt down and cupped his hand, she allowed him to help her into the saddle.

She knew even as she was mounted that the horse responded to her.

She thought she was going to enjoy a really good ride.

She waved to the Captain, who was watching from the Deck.

Then they set off, one man riding ahead to lead the way and the other following behind.

They passed through the dilapidated town and almost immediately were out in the country.

At first there was what appeared to be jungle on either side of the roadway.

Very shortly, however, the trees and shrubs were left behind and the ground appeared to have little vegetation.

She remembered reading that so far as rainfall

was concerned, some parts of Mexico had very wet seasons.

In others the yearly rainfall consisted of not more than a "few drops."

She imagined this applied to Sadaro because it was in the very South of the country.

The ground became more sandy and was flat and perfect for galloping.

Without even discussing it with her escorts, Orina urged her horse forward.

She galloped for over a mile before she drew him in a little.

He was certainly well-trained and broken in, and she settled down to enjoy herself.

She had wanted to see something of the country, and now it lay before her, stretching towards an indefinite horizon where the land met the sky.

There was a slight haze which she knew would disperse when the sun rose higher.

It was already quite warm.

Later in the day she would be glad that she had brought her hat with her.

They rode on and on.

There seemed to be nothing particular to which the men wished to draw her attention.

They must have ridden for nearly two hours before Orina began to think of turning back.

Almost as if they guessed that was what she was thinking, one of the men pointed ahead and said:

"Pyramid—fine Pyramid leetle further on."

His Spanish was strange and obviously mixed with Indian words.

Orina thought she understood and was eager to see a Pyramid.

They rode for a long time, but there was still no sign of it.

"Where is the Pyramid?" she asked, speaking slowly so that they would understand.

"Further—little further," one man replied.

Orina looked up at the sky.

The sun was now very warm.

If she were to be back at the yacht in time for luncheon, she should really turn back now.

"I'll see the Pyramid another day," she said.

"See soon!" the man she addressed answered.

He was looking ahead far into the distance.

Orina thought there was a small dark spot against the unbroken surface of the land.

Because she did not want to disappoint the men who were obviously doing their best to please her, she said:

"Very well, but after that we must go back."

She thought they understood, and she moved her horse a little quicker.

As they drew nearer, she thought the Pyramid looked rather strange.

Eventually, when she could see it more clearly, she realised it was not a Pyramid at all.

It appeared to be a rough-looking Indian house.

"That is not a Pyramid," she exclaimed.

"Food for *Señorita*!" the man replied triumphantly. "Good Mexican food—*Señorita* enjoy!"

Orina looked at him in perplexity.

"You have arranged a meal for me?" she asked.

He recognised the word and smiled.

"*Sí, sí, Señorita*, meal. *Masa!* Very nice—very good!"

It seemed rather strange, Orina thought.

At the same time, it was touching that they should have planned to give her something to eat.

They had certainly brought her a long way to do so.

They reached the house, and it was nothing more than a large hut.

Orina saw that it was occupied by Indians.

There were Indian children playing outside.

There were also a few scraggly hens scratching amongst the cactus, and a Nanny goat tethered to a post.

The two men dismounted and ran to take the bridle of Orina's horse.

She slipped to the ground and watched the horses being led away to the back of the building.

She walked up some rickety steps and in through the door of the hut.

Waiting inside was an Indian woman who bowed low, her hands pressed palm to palm.

She then showed Orina into a room which she was aware occupied half the house.

On the other side she saw what must be the kitchen.

In the room into which she had been shown there was a table in the glassless window.

There was a chair on which she was obviously expected to sit.

The rest of the room was empty except for a large pile of mattresses.

She was sure they would at other times have covered the floor.

Against one wall there was a shrine in which there was the statue of an Indian God.

"This is interesting," Orina said to herself. "Now I have seen a Mexican-Indian house. It is certainly different from the tents in the Arabian desert, or the *tepees* used by our Indians."

The two men had now come into the kitchen.

She could hear them talking and laughing with the Indian woman who appeared to be doing the cooking.

A few minutes later she came into the room, bringing Orina's luncheon.

It was surprisingly edible.

She had heard of *masa*. It started with dried kernels soaked in lime-juice to sweeten them, after which they were ground into a dough called *masa*.

To this was added anything that was available.

Orina was not quite certain what her particular dish contained.

Yet, because she was hungry, she finished up everything in the rough, hand-made dish.

Following was something she had heard was a speciality of Southern Mexico. Little puddings were wrapped in banana leaves, tasting unexpectedly of artichoke.

After that the woman brought her a few fruits.

They were similar to those she had given the children in the town the day before.

She ate one of them, then came a cup of coffee.

This was enjoyable, hot, and fragrant and she drank it slowly.

"This has been very interesting," she told herself, "but I would rather like to have talked to the woman."

She guessed, however, that the woman could speak only her particular brand of Spanish-Indian.

She was obviously getting along well with the two men who were eating in the kitchen.

They laughed continually and she could hear the woman laughing with them.

She finished the coffee, then, when she was about to suggest they should go back, she suddenly felt very tired.

It was a tiredness that swept over her so swiftly that it was difficult to keep her eyes open.

Even as it struck her as very strange and she tried to rise to her feet, she was aware that the Indian woman was beside her.

Then she knew no more.

*   *   *

Orina felt somebody touch her arm.

She thought it was too early to get up.

She was just about to say so when she was aware of a voice saying:

"Wake, *Señorita*, wake!"

She opened her eyes.

For a moment she could not think what had happened to the roof of her cabin.

Then she knew that she was looking at a very different ceiling.

Of rough wood, it had holes in it through which she could see the sky.

"Wake, *Señorita!*"

The woman was speaking again.

As Orina looked up at her she was aware that she was lying on the floor on a mattress.

"What has happened?" she asked. "Why . . . have I . . . been asleep?"

"We must leave, *Señorita*," a man's voice was saying. "The horses are waiting."

She realised the voice belonged to one of the men with whom she had been riding.

With a superhuman effort she sat up.

She rubbed her eyes as she did so and tried to make herself think clearly.

She was still so sleepy that she wanted to lie down again.

The Indian woman handed her a glass containing lime-juice. Orina felt that her mouth was very dry.

She drank thirstily and her mind cleared.

"What time . . . is it?" she asked. "And how can I have gone . . . to sleep?"

"It is very hot, *Señorita*," the man who was standing just inside the door answered. "You tired. We all sleep when sun high in sky."

Orina thought there was some other reason, but she did not feel capable of arguing about it at the moment.

Instead, she rose a little unsteadily to her feet.

Picking up her hat which was beside her on the mattress, she put it on.

Her head seemed lighter. Now she was suspicious that there had been something in the coffee.

It had made her sleep so quickly and so deeply.

She thought perhaps the men wanted to rest.

They had thought like most foreigners she would refuse to obey what was a custom of the country.

"I had better not accuse them of anything," she told herself, "but another time I will be more careful when they offer me a cup of coffee."

She walked towards the door.

Then, taking three silver coins from her pocket, she gave them to the Indian woman.

"*Muchas gracias!*" she said.

The Indian woman bowed deeply and thanked her profusely in her own language.

Orina walked carefully down the broken steps.

The horses were waiting.

She was helped into the saddle and they rode away.

The Indian woman bade them farewell in a shrill, excited voice.

Orina waved to her.

The two men rode off at a quick gallop, and she followed them.

They had gone a little way before Orina suddenly realised they were heading in the opposite direction from which they had come.

They were continuing to go West.

Because she had been drowsy, she had not realised that, as they left the Indian woman, they had not turned Eastwards.

She reined in her horse.

"We are going the wrong way," she said. "I want to return to the yacht!"

"We take *Señorita* by different route," one of the men said.

Orina shook her head.

"No!" she said firmly. "I would rather return the way we came."

She would have turned her horse's head, but both men said quickly:

"No, no, *Señorita*, come this way."

"What is the time?" Orina asked.

She was wishing as she spoke that she had brought her watch with her.

"Plenty time go our way," one of the men insisted.

He urged his horse forward as he spoke, and Orina hesitated.

She was sure it was a mistake to go any farther.

At the same time, she was not certain she could find her way back without them guiding her.

It seemed to her that she had come in a straight line from the sea to the Indian house.

But she could not be certain of it because they had been galloping.

She thought it would be a mistake to be lost in this strange part of the country.

There appeared to be very few inhabitants.

In fact, now that she thought about it, she could not remember seeing any houses since they had left the town.

Nor, for that matter, any people.

There must have been some, but she could not remember exactly.

She had been concentrating on her horse and enjoying the ride.

She had looked ahead rather than from side to side, as she might have done if they had not been travelling so fast.

"Come, *Señorita*, come!"

The men by this time had gone quite a way ahead of her.

Reluctantly, thinking they were being rather tiresome, she rode after them.

She was not certain how to cope.

They rode for about half-an-hour, and now she was convinced they were still going West.

"I must go back to the yacht!" she said firmly. "If I do not, the Captain will send people in search of me. He will also be angry because you have kept me out so long."

She thought one of the men shrugged his shoulders, but could not be certain.

She wondered how best she could impress on them the necessity for taking her back.

Then, just ahead, she saw coming towards her a number of horsemen.

Because they were stirring up a lot of dust, it took Orina time to discern that there were six of them. One man was riding ahead of the others.

They drew nearer, and she was aware that the man riding in front was impressive.

He was definitely different from the other men accompanying him.

They were all riding extremely well, seeming to be a part of their horses.

Because she was a good judge of horsemanship,

Orina knew the man in front was exceptional.

He came towards her at a quick gallop.

Then, just before he reached her, he and the men with him pulled up the horses so that they reared.

This, Orina knew, was an old Arab trick which her father had told her about.

It was surprising, however, to find it in Mexico.

Then she remembered that the Spaniards were famous for being exceptional riders.

As she looked at the leading man approaching her, she wondered who he could be.

He did not seem to fit into either the Spanish or Indian category like the other riders with him.

His skin was brown, which might have been from the sun.

His features were clear-cut. He could have belonged to either race.

But because he was obviously tall and broad-shouldered, she guessed, however, he was a Spaniard rather than an Indian.

She was aware, of course, that even in that race there were tall and powerful men.

The leader then rode his horse slowly forward until he was facing her.

"Good-afternoon, Miss Vandeholt!" he said. "I hope you are rested after the first part of your ride."

He was speaking in English, and Orina stared at him in sheer astonishment.

Whatever she had expected, it was not this.

For a moment she could only stare at him, thinking she could not have heard aright.

He certainly did not look English.

He was casually dressed in a shirt that might have been worn by a working man in almost any country.

His breeches were dilapidated and his boots unpolished.

There was a coloured handkerchief tied at his throat in place of a tie.

He wore a large *sombrero* tipped to one side on his head.

Even as she looked at him, she knew he had an authority about him that was unmistakable.

Whatever his race, he was obviously a leader.

He was waiting for her to reply, and after a long pause Orina found her voice.

"Good afternoon," she replied. "As you know who I am, I would be grateful if you could tell me whether I am heading in the right direction for Sadaro. I wish to get there quickly, but these young men who are escorting me are, I think, taking me the wrong way."

"That is correct, and may I suggest you follow me," the English-speaking man said.

"Thank you," Orina replied.

She thought they would turn back the way they had come.

Instead, he turned his horse round and waited for her to come up beside him.

His followers drew aside for the man and Orina to pass ahead of them.

"I am very interested in seeing this country," she said as they moved off, "but I feel I have gone far enough for one day."

"You have not far to go now," the man beside her replied.

They rode for a while in silence before she asked:

"As you know my name, I would like to know yours."

"It is Juarez," he replied.

He spoke curtly, almost as if he resented the question.

She glanced at him and thought he was certainly a somewhat enigmatic man.

She wanted to ask him how it was that he could speak such good English.

Then, because of the way he had replied to her previous question, she was silent, afraid he would think she was merely being inquisitive.

She remembered that some Mexican people did not like strangers or tourists.

Perhaps that was the way this man felt and was, in fact, going to say that she was trespassing on his land.

They rode on in silence, and the ground became drier and less fertile.

There were no trees, no shrubs, no vegetation of any sort.

She was just about to comment on it when suddenly she saw ahead what seemed to be a huge mountain.

"Surely that is not Sadaro?" she said. "It must be, but it looks very strange from here."

"It is the end of a mountain range," the man riding beside her replied.

"A mountain range?" Orina exclaimed. "But I wish to return to the sea."

"I am afraid that is impossible," Juarez remarked.

She looked at him in astonishment.

"I do not understand."

"Everything will be explained to you as soon as we reach what lies ahead."

Orina drew in her breath.

It struck her that she was being kidnapped.

She thought how stupid she had been not to think of it before.

It had never occurred to her for one moment that she might be in danger of being held for ransom.

Now she asked herself how she could have been so blind.

Of course that was the reason why the men had ridden with her so far and drugged her coffee.

They had been waiting for the arrival of this man, who was the instigator of the plot.

She remembered how careful her father had always been when they were on the Ranch.

There had been guards on duty at night and she never went riding without a groom.

In fact, there were usually two, who, she suspected, although he never said so, were armed.

Yet, because Mexico was an unknown land, she had no idea anybody would be aware of her identity.

It had never crossed her mind that there might be people wishing to kidnap her, knowing what a sensation it would be if it happened in America.

But she was not in the United States.

She was in Mexico, in a strange, uninhabited part of it.

She wondered frantically how she could escape from the men who had taken her prisoner.

Her first impulse was to turn her horse round and make a dash for freedom.

Then she was aware that she had little or no chance of getting away.

There was the man riding beside her and his followers behind.

Their horses were fresher and doubtless swifter than the one she was riding.

She began to be frightened.

Then she told herself that what they wanted was money.

'It may prove an expensive ride, but once I have paid up, I shall be able to return to the yacht.'

Riding in silence, they drew nearer to what she now saw was a stony mountain range without any vegetation.

It was high in some places, lower in others.

As they drew nearer, she saw to her astonishment that waiting on ground just below the mountain were many people, more people than she had ever expected to see in the land through which she had passed.

There were women and children and roughly made tents and shelters.

These comprised little more than pieces of cloth raised on sticks.

In some cases, bamboo had been stripped and plaited into some form of roof.

At first Orina looked round her in bewilderment, thinking there must be more than a thousand people there.

Then the crowd saw the horses coming and they shouted and waved to the man at whose side she was riding.

He raised his hand in a half-salute, and there was a faint smile on his lips.

It made him seem not quite so formidable as he had done before.

At the same time, Orina knew that he was frightening.

Despite what she hoped was an air of self-assurance, she was actually very nervous.

'I will pay anything he demands,' she thought, 'but only on condition that he sets me free immediately!'

The horses made their way through the crowd of people squatting on the ground.

Then they wound their way through stones and boulders until they reached the foot of the mountain.

Orina then saw there were huge holes in the rock surface, and she knew they were caves.

When finally the horses came to a standstill, she saw they were beside some roughly hewn steps.

Juarez dismounted and came forward to take the bridle of Orina's horse.

Without being ordered to do so, she slipped to the ground.

Juarez handed the bridle to another man and said curtly:

"Follow me!"

He walked ahead up the steps, and Orina followed him.

She did not look back.

Yet she had the uncomfortable feeling that his followers, who had hardly spoken a word since they left the house of the Indian woman, were watching.

She knew now that the men who had brought her from the yacht had been told to tempt her yesterday by showing her their horses.

They must be congratulating themselves on carrying out their orders so efficiently.

She felt a sudden hatred rise within her because they had so cleverly deceived her.

She had been too foolish not to realise they were impostors.

"I did not use my perception as Papa taught me to do," she told herself.

Juarez was still climbing.

At last they reached a small platform, and she saw in front of her a wide opening into what she knew was a cave.

They went into it, and before she followed him, Orina looked back.

Now she could see in the distance the way they had come over the barren, infertile land.

There was directly below them the crowd of people camping in front of the mountains.

There seemed to be even more now than she had thought as they rode through them.

She asked herself why they were there.

Then, because she was aware without him speaking that Juarez was waiting for her inside, she went into the cave.

It was far bigger than she expected; it was, in fact, as large as a room in any ordinary house.

It was sparsely furnished with two or three armchairs.

There was a long table which was being used as a desk, and there were carpets on the floor.

She recognised them as being made by the natives from sheep's wool and dyed with vegetable dyes.

Juarez had taken off his *sombrero* and was now standing, waiting for her.

He looked not, as she might have expected, disreputable in his tattered clothing, but authoritative.

Also, as Orina was aware, he was very sure of himself.

Because she was determined to take the initiative, she said:

"You might as well tell me straight away what ransom you require, as I am prepared to pay it. Then I ask you to take me back as quickly as possible to my yacht."

"I thought you would realise that I needed a ransom for you," Juarez said.

"It is something I should have been aware of before," Orina answered, "and I can only blame myself for being so stupid as to trust any man, whatever his nationality."

She spoke scathingly, hoping he would realise she was not to be intimidated by him.

"I see you are taking this very sensibly," he

said, "and so I will explain as briefly as possible why I have brought you here."

"I have already realised that," Orina said. "Once again, as it will save time, I ask you to tell me how much you require."

He smiled before he said:

"Suppose you sit down?"

"I think that is quite unnecessary," Orina answered. "The matter is just one of business, and the sooner you tell me the exact sum, I will inform you how it can be paid and the whole matter can be closed."

She thought as she spoke that her father would have been proud of her.

She was doing a business deal in a businesslike manner and she hoped the man facing her would realise her competence.

Instead, to her annoyance, he pulled forward an upright chair and set it down in front of the table.

Then he walked round it to sit down so that he was facing her.

"Now, Miss Vandeholt, if that is what you wish, we can talk business."

"That is what I want," Orina said, "and as I have already told you, I must return to my yacht as quickly as possible."

Juarez sighed.

"I am afraid that will be impossible!"

"What do you mean—impossible?" Orina asked sharply.

"You must allow me to explain this in my own words," he said, "which will actually save a great deal of time."

"Very well," Orina conceded, "but please, do not make it too long-winded."

She forced herself to sit back in her chair and appear at her ease.

Yet, because her head was aching a little, she pulled off her hat and impatiently put it down on the floor.

"You have, of course, seen those people sitting outside—through whom we have just passed?" Juarez began.

"Yes, yes, of course I saw them!" Orina snapped. "What have they to do with me?"

"A great deal," he answered, "because they are starving."

"Starving?" Orina exclaimed. "But why?"

"Because there has been no rain in this part of the country for nearly two years. This is their home—this is where they have lived for so many centuries that it is impossible for anyone to know how long."

He paused before he went on:

"They are a tribe which are gradually becoming extinct simply through starvation, but this year things are worse than they have ever been, and somebody has to do something about it."

"Which, I suppose, is you!" Orina said sarcastically.

"Exactly," he replied, "but, unfortunately, I have not the money to do what I want, and that, Miss Vandeholt, is where you come in."

"As I have already told you, I will pay the ransom you require. I cannot imagine why you do not tell me exactly how much that entails so that

I can return before dark, otherwise the Captain of my yacht will undoubtedly be worried and make every effort to find me."

"I understand," Juarez said, "and therefore to put it in as few words as possible, I want to help these people by bringing them water."

Orina stared at him.

"Bring them water? What do you mean by that?"

"It is possible, I have discovered," he explained, "to bring water across these mountains by building a dam to fill this valley from a stream that is otherwise lost in the other direction. It has just been flowing away and is of no use to anyone."

"It sounds like a very clever idea!" Orina said. "And I understand you would need quite a lot of money to finance it. Very well—how much?"

"That is something that is impossible to estimate, even with expert advice," Juarez said. "That means I need to budget for today and tomorrow, and for the future."

Orina drew in her breath.

She was thinking his demand was going to be extraordinarily large, in which case it might be difficult to persuade her father's lawyers to pay it.

"I know what you are thinking," Juarez said unexpectedly, "and of course you are right. That is why, Miss Vandeholt, I realise that if my dam and the work I have to do can be carried out, and save the lives of these people, there is only one way by which it can be accomplished."

He waited without speaking, as if forcing her

to ask the question he was waiting to hear.

"And how is that?" she asked at length, reluctantly.

"That you marry me!" he replied.

chapter five

ORINA stared at him.

Her eyes seemed to fill her whole face.

"Is this a joke?" she asked.

"Certainly not!" Juarez replied. "But it is the only way by which I can obtain the money I want."

Orina drew in her breath.

"I have already offered you any money you need," she said slowly, as if he were being particularly stupid.

"And find myself arrested on a charge of kidnapping for the extortion of money?" he replied. "That is a serious offence in Mexico and means about ten years in prison."

Orina began to feel frightened.

"I am sure we can arrange something in a satisfactory manner," she said at length.

"On the contrary," Juarez replied, "the only thing which will make me sure of finishing my dam and saving the lives of those people out there is if you are my wife!"

"Which I refuse . . . absolutely . . . refuse to . . . be!" Orina replied.

"There is, I suppose, an alternative," he said slowly.

"And . . . what is . . . that?"

She tried to speak defiantly, but she had the feeling that her voice was rather weak.

She wondered if it was because of the drug that had been put in her coffee.

"I can make you mine," Juarez said, "and if I give you a child and you still refuse to marry me, then I can fight in the Courts for the custody of it on the grounds that you are not a fit mother, as you would not accept my offer of marriage."

He spoke in a dry, businesslike manner, but Orina felt as if he menaced her like a savage animal.

She was trying to think of what she should say.

At the same time, her father had taught her to think quickly and objectively.

She knew that if she was honest, his argument was irrefutable.

"I will . . . not marry you! I will . . . not!" she cried.

"In point of fact," Juarez said quietly, "we are already married!"

"W-what do you . . . mean by . . . that?"

"Yesterday, when I saw you in Sadaro," he said, "I knew that you were my only hope and

I therefore made quite certain that you could not escape."

"I . . . I do not know what . . . you are . . . saying."

"Then let me explain it," he said. "I went into Sadaro to make a last fervent plea to obtain a grant from the Governor. He was, as usual, drunk, and he made it quite clear that any money he had to spend in this Province would be spent on his comfort."

Orina knew that was why Government House looked so different from the dilapidated houses around it.

"In despair I went to see a Priest," Juarez was saying. "He has supported me in every way he can since I started trying to save the people outside from starvation. He is aware that I have spent every penny of my own money and everything else that I could beg or borrow from every friend I ever had."

He spoke quietly, without bitterness, and, as Orina did not speak, he went on:

"As I was leaving his house I saw you giving fruit to the children and I asked a young girl to find out who you were. When she told me, I went to the yacht and attempted to see you."

Orina remembered how she had sent the caller away, being eager to read her book.

"I thought when I got your message," Juarez said, "that you were just like all other American women—spoilt, selfish, unsympathetic, concerned only with your own interests and no one else's."

Now he spoke so scathingly that Orina felt as if he whipped her with his words.

"That is . . . not true—" she tried to say.

But he interrupted:

"I went back to my friend the Priest and told him what I intended, and we went at once to the Government Office. By the laws of Mexico, anyone can get married who produces the right documents, and it is possible for anyone in authority to stand proxy for the bride."

Orina clenched her fingers together.

She wanted to scream, but Juarez went on:

"I have raised a Letter of Credit for you at the local Bank and all you have to do now is to write a cheque which will pay for the food which arrives every three days to feed these people."

He sighed before he went on:

"The food which is arriving to-day is the last they will deliver without further payment."

He got up as he spoke and walked to the open window.

Almost as if she were hypnotised and could not think for herself, Orina followed him.

She saw that since they had been talking, a huge wagon drawn by six horses had pulled into the centre of the crowd.

Bags which she knew contained grain were being distributed into the eager hands of the women.

The children were clustering round, wide-eyed.

They were obviously excited at the thought of the food they would have as soon as it was cooked.

"You heard me say that was the last consignment they will send without further money," Juarez said. "If your cheque does not go back with the wagon, there will be a delay of at least twenty-four hours."

Now there was a note in his voice which told Orina how much it meant to him, also how determined he was to have his own way.

"I will write you a cheque for anything you want," she said, "but I will still not agree to marry you."

"Write the cheque."

He went back to the table and produced a cheque-book which she had never seen before.

She realised it was on the Bank of Sadaro, where he had obviously opened an account for her.

Disdainfully, because she was hating him with a violence that she had never felt before, she said:

"You had . . . better make it out and I will . . . sign it."

He did not argue, he merely filled in a sum at which she deliberately did not look.

When he had done so, he pushed it across the table towards her.

"You will sign it," he said, "as Orina Standish."

"Standish?" she questioned. "Then you are English?"

"When I came here," he replied, "and told the people my name, they thought I said 'Juarez,' who is one of their heroes."

"So you did not correct them?"

"Why should I?" he answered. "It made me learn to get my own way."

Orina thought, however, she had heard the name when she was in England.

She looked at the cheque.

"I refuse to sign it except with my own name," she said.

He looked at her across the table.

"I can make you do as I want," he said, "but you may find it extremely painful."

Not only what he said, but the way he looked at her, told her she dare not go too far.

She was completely helpless in the hands of this madman.

She was sure he would do anything to save the people outside.

For a moment she met his eyes defiantly.

Then, because she was afraid, she picked up the pen.

She signed the cheque.

Without speaking he picked it up and, going to the opening of the cave, called to a man who was waiting outside.

He spoke to him in Spanish.

Orina understood what he said and knew he gave instructions for the man to give it to the driver of the wagon.

He was to say that they would expect another consignment of food on Friday.

The man hurried away and Juarez came back.

"We are being married in two hours time, after my people have eaten," he said. "They are looking forward excitedly to the ceremonies."

"Do you really . . . think that I . . . will make a . . . 'Peep-Show' of myself to . . . amuse that . . .

rabble?" Orina asked angrily. "I can speak Spanish. Suppose I tell them what . . . you are doing . . . to me . . . and how . . . intolerably you are . . . behaving?"

"Those who speak Spanish will not believe you," Juarez said coolly, "and the majority are Indians who will not understand you."

There was silence, then Orina said:

"Please . . . please do not do . . . this to me! I will give you any . . . money you . . . want. I will . . . pretend to be . . . your . . . wife until you let me go . . . but I hate all men . . . how then can . . . you wish to . . . marry me?"

"I thought I had made myself clear—I am interested in your money—not in you!" Juarez replied. "As long as you do what I want, you will be perfectly safe. Then when I let you return to civilisation you can doubtless pay enough to have our marriage annulled, or ask for a divorce."

Orina shut her eyes.

He had an answer to everything. She had to concede that he had thought out every detail to his own advantage.

Once again she wanted to scream, but the self-control her father had taught her, and her pride, made her merely hold her head high.

But her fingers were still clenched.

Unexpectedly, he said in a quieter, more gentle manner:

"I suggest you now go and rest. An Indian girl called Zeeti, who speaks a little English, will look after you. I have provided you with a gown that is suitable as a wedding-dress."

Quite suddenly Orina again felt rebellious.

"I will not have you dictating what I shall wear at this ceremony which is nothing but a mockery! I will appear because you make me, but in what I have on at the moment."

"That will be very disappointing for the people who are waiting for us," Juarez said, "and as your riding-clothes are dusty, and you are doubtless hot after being in the saddle for most of the day, I suggest you wash yourself before putting on the clean gown which I have obtained for you."

The way he spoke made her more angry than she was already.

Before she could shout at him that she would do nothing of the sort, however, he added:

"Of course, if you need my assistance, I am prepared to help you undress."

There was no doubt now of the threat in his voice, and Orina retorted furiously:

"How can you be so brutal . . . so appalling! You pose as a benefactor to all these people, but I personally believe you are . . . the Devil himself!"

Juarez threw back his head and laughed.

"I think few people here would agree with you," he said. "If I am, in your opinion, the Devil, then I am quite prepared to behave like him. So be a good girl and do as you are told. It is quite useless to oppose me. As you would know if you troubled to use your brain, I hold all the cards."

Orina wanted to strike him.

Instead, she turned round and walked towards the opening of the cave.

It was covered by a curtain which he had pulled into place when they entered.

She dragged it back, feeling she must run away and try, hopeless though it seemed, to escape from him.

Then Juarez said again in the same businesslike voice he had used before:

"There is no need to go outside. Our sleeping quarters open out of this cave, which makes it more convenient."

Orina could see the people taking the sacks from the wagon, which was now practically empty.

Then, as she looked down the steps up which they had come, she saw that half-way down there was a man standing as if on guard.

She knew without being told that if she tried to pass him, he would prevent her from doing so.

Helplessly she turned back to see that Juarez was at the end of the cave, where there was another curtain.

He pulled it to one side.

She saw that it opened into a smaller cave which she knew without being told was her bed-room.

There was a bed that was more like an Oriental couch, only a little raised off the floor.

Light was coming from another unpaned opening.

It was too high off the ground to be able to see out of it.

It occurred to her that if one could not look out, it was impossible for anyone to look in.

That, she supposed, was an advantage.

"This will be your room," Juarez was saying, "and it may be a comfort for you to know that mine is on the other side of the cave we have just left."

She thought he spoke mockingly.

Her chin went up and she stiffened.

But before she could speak, a woman came in through the door through which they had just entered.

"This is Zeeti," Juarez said, "and, as I told you, she understands a little English."

Zeeti was an Indian girl and was, Orina thought, very pretty.

She made Orina a deep obeisance with her hands pressed together in the Indian manner of greeting.

"I . . . look . . . after . . . *Señorita*," she said in hesitating English.

"Thank you," Orina said.

"Your clothes will be coming to-morrow," Juarez said.

"My clothes?" Orina repeated stupidly.

"I forgot to tell you," he replied, "that you sent a letter to your Captain after your *siesta* telling him you had met some friends with whom you were staying. You told him to despatch all the clothes you would require for the next two or three weeks in a vehicle which will call at the yacht early to-morrow morning."

"I wrote . . . a letter? What do you . . . mean by . . . that?" Orina asked. "If you have . . . forged my . . . signature he will not be . . . taken in . . . by it!"

"The Priest is a very erudite man who can copy anyone's hand-writing so exactly that I very much doubt if the Captain will not accept it as coming from you."

Orina looked at him. Then she said slowly:

"The girl . . . who made me sign my name when I was in the village!"

"Exactly!" Juarez replied. "That is also why the Letter of Credit will be accepted in New York."

"*You* sent her!" Orina said accusingly.

"When I organise anything," he replied, "I think of every detail, and being a woman, you would naturally want clothes, even if there is no one but myself to appreciate them."

He was deliberately provoking her, Orina thought, and although she wanted to rage at him, again she controlled herself.

He waited.

Then, as he realised she would not be drawn, he turned with what she thought was an unpleasant smile on his lips to leave the cave.

As he reached the opening, he spoke to Zeeti in an Indian language which Orina did not understand.

Then he was gone and she sank down on a chair.

Her fingers felt stiff from having clenched them for so long.

"*Señorita* have shower?" Zeeti asked in a humble little voice.

"A shower?" Orina exclaimed in surprise.

The Indian girl nodded and, going to the entrance, beckoned.

Orina followed her slowly.

She was afraid Juarez would still be waiting there.

But the big cave was empty and Zeeti took her to another hole in the wall.

This, too, was covered on the inside with a curtain.

As the girl pulled it back, Orina saw that it was made of some waterproof material.

Inside there was what appeared to be an empty cave with a very small opening to let in the light.

Then Orina saw that up near the roof there was a wooden platform on which stood two buckets.

There was a hole in the ground through which the water could flow away.

It doubtless ran down the side of the mountain.

Because it was so primitive, and in a way so funny, Orina could not help giving a little laugh.

"It is very clever!"

"Como Dios like very much."

"Como Dios?" Orina repeated slowly. " 'Like God'—is that what you call him?"

Zeeti nodded.

"Como Dios very . . . great man. Save our . . . lives. Save many . . . many children. To us he come with . . . name of hero, but we know . . . he like God."

'He is certainly not like God to me!' Orina wanted to say.

Then she knew it would be a mistake.

Instead, she went back to her own cave and started to undress.

She was aware as she did so that Juarez was right and her riding-clothes were thick with dust.

Zeeti poured the bucket of water over her.

She allowed her only one bucketful, because the other had to be kept for *Como Dios*.

Then she wrapped Orina in a sheet and took her back to her own cave without her seeing anyone.

She got into bed.

She was worn out after her long ride, the coffee that had been drugged, and the emotions of the last hour.

She fell asleep.

*   *   *

Orina awoke to find Zeeti was kneeling humbly beside her.

"Time you dress, *Señorita*," she said.

Orina rubbed her eyes.

She felt better than she had when she lay down.

She thought she must have slept for over an hour.

There was still light coming through what she was to think of as "her window."

But she was aware the sun would be sinking over the horizon.

Zeeti helped her into an under-garment, then produced the gown of which Juarez had spoken.

Orina realised at once that it was made in the classical Indian fashion.

She had seen it in photographs and engravings of the statues and the reliefs which had been found in the Pyramids.

The gown was of a soft white material, but it was held only by a string across her breasts.

Her neck and shoulders were bare.

It had a sash round the waist and it reached to the ground, where it was embroidered round the hem.

Red and green leaves were, she knew, the primitive colours with which the Mexican Indians decorated their rugs.

She had seen them already on the floor in the outer cave.

There was no veil, but Zeeti produced a wreath.

It was made of leaves that might have come from the same shrub as those that decorated the hem of the gown.

She had loosened her hair when she undressed.

Zeeti produced a brush and left it flowing over her shoulders.

It was very long; in fact, it nearly reached her waist.

Just for a moment Orina thought of protesting and pinning it up as it had been when she arrived.

Then she told herself that it hid the nakedness of her shoulders and she said nothing.

"*Señorita* very pretty . . . very beautiful. *Como Dios* pleased."

Orina wanted to retort that the last thing she wished to do was to please "*Como Dios*."

But she knew the Indian girl would not understand.

Also she thought it vulgar to discuss her personal feelings with anyone, least of all a strange girl who obviously adored the man who was behaving in such an outrageous manner.

Now she was dressed and she knew in a moment she would have to go to him.

She felt a sudden panic sweep over her.

"What can . . . I do? Oh . . . God . . . what can . . . I do?" she asked. "How can I . . . marry this man? How can I be . . . humiliated by . . . him just . . . because he . . . wants my money?"

She wondered if she should throw herself down on her bed and pretend to be unconscious.

Then she remembered how menacing he had been when he said he would undress her.

She knew she was too frightened to disobey him.

Zeeti peeped through the curtains that were drawn over the opening into the outer cave.

There was a delighted smile on her lips as she said:

"He waiting . . . ready for you . . . *Sēnorita*! I wish you very happy."

As she spoke she went down on her knees and kissed Orina's hand.

Because she could think of nothing to say, Orina walked with what she hoped was pride and dignity into the larger cave.

For a moment she could only stare at Juarez.

He certainly looked very different from when she had last seen him.

Now he was wearing the clothes of a *gaucho* and nothing could be more becoming.

His pleated white shirt, his short black jacket, the long, tapering trousers, and red cummerbund made him seem taller, also more overwhelming than he had seemed before.

His hair was still wet from his shower. Where before it had been tousled and untidy, it was now brushed smoothly to his head.

For a moment they just stared at each other. Then he said:

"I suppose I should tell you that you look very beautiful."

Orina knew he was being sarcastic.

She merely replied coldly in French so that Zeeti would not understand:

"I think it would be a mistake to quarrel in front of the servants."

Her answer obviously surprised him.

"Touché!" he exclaimed.

His eyes were undoubtedly twinkling.

Then he offered her his arm and she put her hand lightly on it as they went through the outer opening.

The people were waiting, and she saw their faces raised towards them.

She realised how excited they were.

At their appearance, a great shout went up that seemed to ring out and fill the air.

As Orina had anticipated, the sun was sinking.

The sky was crimson on the horizon, but was still clear just above them.

Juarez acknowledged the cheers by raising his arm.

With the people still cheering, they went slowly down the steps.

As they reached the ground, the crowd opened so that they could pass between them.

The children danced ahead and ran beside them.

They were saying things in the Indian language which Orina sensed were wishes of Good Luck.

It was then she saw a platform ahead.

On it stood two men.

"I should have told you before," Juarez explained, "we are being married twice."

"Twice?" Orina questioned.

"I have been baptised a Catholic," he said, "and Father Miguel will marry us according to the Catholic rites. It will be a short Service as you are not of the Faith."

"And the other man?" Orina asked.

"The Indians here worship Quetzalcoatl. You have heard of him?"

"I was . . . reading about him . . . when I was on . . . the yacht," Orina replied.

"He is the God of Wind, of Life, and of the Morning Star."

Juarez said that many of the Pyramids and caves found in this part of the country were dedicated to him, and used in his worship.

Orina was silent.

She could not believe what was happening.

She was to be married to a man she hated by the Rites of the Catholic Church, in which marriage was a Sacrament.

She was also to be married by a Priest who had dedicated himself to Quetzalcoatl, one of the greatest of the Indian Gods, but a Pagan Deity.

They reached the platform.

Now Orina could see that behind the Catholic Priest there was a small altar.

On it there was a crucifix and a flat stone.

Orina knew that this was the Consecration Stone which was carried by all Missionaries who moved about the country.

Her father had once pointed one out in the backwoods of the North-West.

There was no Church for the people who lived there.

They therefore relied entirely on visiting Priests.

Orina and Juarez stood in front of the altar. The people were silent.

They were listening attentively to the Service.

The prayers were in Spanish, then in Latin.

It was not difficult for Orina to follow what was happening.

For the first time she heard the names of the man she was marrying.

Alexis Louis took her to be his lawful wedded wife and put the wedding-ring on her finger.

She was not surprised he had one.

She only thought it was either very clever on his part, or sheer good luck that it fitted.

They knelt and received the Blessing.

She tried to tell herself it was just a mockery because of the terrible way she was being married.

Yet she could not help hoping that God would bless her and things would not be as bad as they seemed.

Then as the Priest, an elderly man with a beard, turned round to kneel at the Altar, Juarez took her hand.

Drawing her to her feet, he led her to the other side of the platform.

The Indian was a tall man who had, Orina thought, a singularly arresting, if rugged, face.

He began to speak in a quiet, deep voice.

As he did so, Juarez translated in little more than a whisper what he was saying—

"Barefoot on the living earth with faces to the living sun, a man and a woman in the presence of the Morning Star meet to be perfect in one another."

Because the words were so beautiful, Orina found herself listening, mesmerised.

The Indian Priest was still speaking, and Juarez went on:

"Lift your face and say: 'This man is my rain from Heaven.'"

Remembering that Quetzalcoatl was the God of Rain, Orina lifted her face and repeated:

" 'This man is my rain from Heaven.' "

The Indian looked now at Juarez.

"Kneel, *Señor*, touch the earth, and say: 'This woman is the earth to me.' "

Juarez knelt on one knee and laid his hands on the earth, saying:

" 'This woman is the earth to me.' "

He rose and the Indian pointed to Orina.

Following Juarez's whispered instructions, she said slowly:

"I, woman, kiss the feet of . . . this man. I will give . . . strength to him and we shall be . . . one throughout the long . . . twilight and . . . the Morning Star."

"You must kneel," Juarez whispered.

For a moment she wanted to defy him.

Then she could feel the vibrations coming from all the Indians who were pressing around them.

She was aware they were deeply moved, and the Service meant something very sacred to them.

She did not know how or why she was completely convinced of this, but she could feel it in her mind and, strangely enough, in her heart.

Therefore, without feeling she was humiliating herself by doing so, she knelt and bowed her head.

"You must kiss my feet," Juarez said very softly. "First one, then the other."

Orina shut her eyes.

She did not actually kiss his shining boots.

She bent over them in the way a Frenchman would bend over a woman's hand.

Then she felt Juarez touch her hair and say, now speaking in English:

"I, man, kiss the brow and touch the head of this woman. I will be her peace and her rescue, and we shall be one in the long twilight and the Morning Star."

He spoke the words very movingly.

Then he raised Orina to her feet and, bending forward, kissed her forehead.

When he had done so, the Priest put Juarez's hand over Orina's eyes and her hand over his and said:

"This man has met this woman with his body and the Star of his shape, and this woman has met this man with her body and the Star of her yearning and they are one, and Quetzalcoatl has blessed them and made them one with the Morning Star."

As Juarez translated the last words, he took away his hand from Orina's eyes and she took hers from his.

As they did so, the last rays of the sunshine seemed to move across the sky.

It enveloped them with an indescribable magic.

Orina could feel it, she could see it.

As if the people were aware of it, too, they suddenly raised their voices in a great cry.

It was clear and sprang from them spontaneously to swell up into the sky.

Then, as both Juarez and Orina stood without moving, the Indian Priest threw back his head.

He raised both his arms as the sun sank below the horizon.

Then there was just the twilight, and the first evening star appeared in the sky above them.

Juarez turned round and offered Orina his arm.

As they started to walk back the way they had come, the people went mad.

They danced, shouted, and raised their hands.

Orina knew that if there had been flowers instead of the barren ground, they would have strewn them in their path.

With some difficulty they reached the steps.

Juarez went up them slowly, stopping on almost every one to wave and acknowledge the cheers.

There was cry after cry of wild excitement from the people.

Having reached the top step, Juarez and Orina stood there for a long time waving and smiling.

At last Juarez drew Orina into the cave.

While they had been away, a small table had been set in the centre of it.

On it there were four lighted candles.

The writing-desk had been laid to act as a side-board.

There was food and a bottle of strange, clear wine.

As Orina stared in surprise, Juarez said:

"I am afraid we must wait on ourselves. Everybody is far too excited not to want to join the crowd who will be dancing and singing for some hours."

As Juarez spoke the sound of music could be heard.

It was unlike any music that Orina recognised.

She knew that it was Indian music.

Although it sounded strange to her, it was mysterious and had something exciting about it.

Despite herself, she had been moved by the two Services in which she had just taken part.

She had prayed to God to save her and show her a means of escape from the man who was forcing himself upon her as her husband.

Orina had knelt in front of the Indian and had taken part in the Service to Quetzalcoatl.

It was either the words themselves or the vibrations of people around her which had moved her emotionally.

She could not help being swept up into a feeling of sanctity which was very different from what she had expected.

Perhaps it had been the Indian's voice.

Perhaps the strange evening sunlight was Quetzalcoatl himself bringing them the Light of the Morning Star.

Now, as she sat down at the table, she told herself she was being mesmerised.

She had been taken into a world to which she did not belong.

"The sooner I return to sanity the better," she murmured beneath her breath.

Juarez poured the strange, clear wine into a beaker and set it down beside her.

"Of course," he said, "on such an auspicious occasion, we must drink to our happiness and, having received the blessings of two different religions, could we expect anything else?"

He was speaking mockingly.

As she picked up her beaker she knew that she hated him with a violence that swept away every other emotion.

She tried to think of something scathing and, if possible, hurtful with which to reply.

But the words would not come.

Instead, she remained silent.

She told herself that whatever Blessing she may have received from the Gods, she was now in the hands of the Devil.

chapter six

IT was only just dawn.

Orina could hear the men singing as they moved off up the mountain to work on the dam.

Juarez had taken her there yesterday, the day after they were married.

She had been astonished at what she saw.

"You are doubtless curious," he had said in his hard, businesslike voice, "as to how your money will be spent. So come with me and I will show you."

It meant rising very early, because the men worked best in the cool of the day.

As she climbed up the side of the mountain, she thought, if nothing else, it was a new experience.

When she reached the top of what was actually a low peak, she saw something which she knew would have thrilled her father.

Juarez had already, with what money he could provide himself, changed the course of a stream.

It came from the mountain and apparently had once flowed into the valley.

Unfortunately, owing to an earthquake, its course had been changed.

Now it fell over the other side of the mountain over a profusion of rocks.

With an expertise she had not expected, Juarez had managed to direct the cascade itself into a stream.

It would in a very short time flow into the dam he was constructing, and from there into the valley.

It was odd, she thought, to find so high a stream.

However, Juarez told her it was not unusual in the mountains of Mexico.

To those living on the East side of the mountains, the loss of it had meant starvation and death.

Looking down at the people encamped below, Orina could see where the original bed of the stream had been.

It had run from the mountain right across the valley towards Sadaro, making the land on each side of it fertile.

Juarez told her exactly what he was planning.

She learnt that the men with him, both Spaniards and Indians, were all working without payment.

Juarez was giving them only Love and the belief that they and their families would live.

They would not have to move from the land they had inhabited for centuries.

"In fact," Juarez said to Orina, "they will not move. They believe they have a right to this place and nothing will persuade them to go anywhere else."

"They would rather die than leave?" Orina asked.

"That sums it up exactly," he replied. "At the same time, if they went anywhere else, they would feel themselves alien and unwanted."

The day after she had been married, Orina received her clothes.

With them came a pleasant letter from Captain Bennett saying he was so glad she had found friends.

He would, of course, wait in Sadaro until he heard from her again.

Juarez had certainly tied things up very cleverly, she thought.

She was, however, glad to have her own dresses.

As it was very hot, she needed something thin and loose to wear when she left the cave.

She soon realised that she was not to be allowed to go anywhere unaccompanied.

There was always somebody on guard to follow her wherever she went, and to listen to whoever she spoke to.

Once again Juarez was being practical in that her guards were elderly men unable to work on the dam.

It made her feel constrained and imprisoned.

She longed to think of some means by which she could escape and make Juarez look foolish.

When he came back in the evenings he was obviously tired.

But he showered and changed into his *gaucho* clothes for dinner.

Because he changed, it made Orina change too, although she disliked making herself, as she put it, "look attractive" for him.

At the same time, she was aware that he did not appear to pay any attention to her as a woman.

When they talked at dinner on various subjects, he invariably took the opposite view from hers.

He seemed to delight in provoking her.

"I hate him!" she told herself a dozen times a day.

Yet she was wise enough not to disparage him in any way to the people he was helping.

They obviously worshipped him.

She found that, like Zeeti, they all spoke of him as *Como Dios*.

She was sure that the followers of Quetzalcoatl believed he was the reincarnation of the famous God.

Juarez was, she learnt, a great hero, yet she knew nothing about him.

She had asked Juarez on the fourth night why he had championed these people.

Although she disliked the word, she was aware he had dedicated himself to assisting them.

For a moment she thought he was not going to answer her.

Then he said:

"When I saw their plight and realised what could be done to save them, I found it impossible,

114

like the Pharisee, to 'pass by on the other side.' "

"My father would have felt the same," Orina said reluctantly.

"But he would have been able to afford to do it without taking the desperate action of marrying you," Juarez replied.

"That was not true when he was young," Orina contradicted Juarez. "He had, in fact, very little money of his own, and only when my grandfather died did he come into possessions which he multiplied and enlarged until he became a very rich man in his desire *to help America*."

She accentuated the last words.

Juarez looked up and asked:

"Is that true? Was he really doing it for idealistic reasons rather than a personal one?"

"If you had known my father, you would have realised how insulted he would have been to be thought he was making money only for money's sake!" Orina replied angrily.

She tried to speak calmly as she went on:

"What he wanted was to make America great, not by fighting for land or possessions, but by producing machinery, ships, railways, and new inventions which would enrich not only his own country, but the whole world."

She spoke with so much emotion that she felt the tears come into her eyes.

She thought that if Juarez did not believe her, or mocked what she was saying, she would throw something at him.

Instead, to her surprise, he said quietly:

"Is that what you intend to do?"

"I am trying—of course I am trying!" Orina answered. "But I am a woman in a man's world, and it will not be easy."

He did not answer.

Because she felt she was going to cry, she left him alone in the big cave and went to her own.

Now, this morning, as she walked down the steps into the sunshine, she felt light-hearted.

Then she wondered how long she was to be isolated here.

She had to find out what was happening to her father's possessions in the United States.

'I must be in touch with Bernard Hoffman,' she thought, 'but how can I explain, even to him, that I am only a "provider of money" for a mad scheme to save a thousand people, instead of concentrating on millions?'

He would be astounded that she was married. He would be sure she could somehow have refused to take part in the ceremonies.

Thoughts of her weakness made her cross and, reaching the bottom of the steps, she walked quickly through the families encamped around her.

The mothers were nursing their babies; the older children were running about laughing and shouting at each other.

Orina was aware that because Juarez was now able to pay for more and better food, the children were stronger and more noisy.

"When I first came here," he related to her, "they would lie beside their parents and just stare into space, or whimper because they were hungry."

Orina tried not to listen to the way he spoke.

She told herself he was only trying to persuade her that he had done the right thing in marrying her.

"He is abominable, appalling, uncivilised!" she raged.

Every time she saw the flash of the ring on her finger she wanted to scream.

She moved among the people, knowing that her guard was not far behind.

Because it was a lovely morning, she walked farther than she usually did. She walked on and now came to the end of the curious-looking shelters which they had erected to protect themselves.

They were needed more for protection from the sun than anything else.

It was then Orina was aware that there were several new-comers.

They were unprotected, on the outskirts of the crowd.

Because their belongings were still done up in bundles, she knew they must have just arrived.

She remembered Juarez had said that the desolation and lack of water covered a large area.

This meant that people were arriving who had heard miles away that food was available near to the mountain.

Orina could see that the new people looked very exhausted.

She wondered if they were aware they could obtain food and also, which was more important, water.

Juarez had laid a long pipe from the stream which came from the mountain.

It came down into the valley where the people were encamped.

There was always a bucket at the bottom of it, but it took a long time to fill.

As soon as it was full, somebody replaced it with another, and the water was distributed.

Orina went up to the new-comers.

One family consisted of a man, who she thought would be able to work on the dam, and a young woman who was holding a baby in her arms.

She saw they were Spanish.

Speaking to them in their own language, she said gently:

"I think you have just arrived. If you need food, you will find it over there at the foot of the mountain."

She pointed to what was left of the last load.

It was guarded day and night by elderly men whom Juarez trusted.

"We walk a long way, *Señora*," the man replied. "My wife very tired."

"I will stay with her while you go and fetch some food," Orina said. "Take a utensil with you and also one for some water."

He searched through the bundles he had been carrying, found what was necessary, and hurried away.

Orina sat down on the sand beside the young woman.

As she did so, she saw how pale she was. Her eyes were half-closed, as if she wished to sleep.

"Let me hold the baby," Orina suggested, reaching out her arms.

She took the baby from the woman and saw that it was a boy.

He had large eyes and long lashes that were characteristic of Spanish children.

But he was very thin.

She was certain that if the mother needed food, the baby needed milk.

She thought that perhaps its mother had found it difficult to feed it on the journey.

She was, however, too shy to ask questions.

Now that she was free of her baby, the mother lay down on the ground.

She put her head on one of the bundles which her husband had left beside her and closed her eyes.

The baby began to whimper.

Orina rose to her feet so that it was easier for her to rock him in her arms.

As she moved about, she was hoping that the man would not be long.

The mother did not move and Orina walked up and down until at last she saw the man returning.

He was walking carefully so as not to spill the water that was contained in a rough pot.

The baby was still whimpering and, as he reached her, Orina asked:

"Have you some food for the baby?"

"My wife will feed him," he replied.

He put what he carried down on the ground beside his wife and tried to waken her.

Then suddenly he gave a loud cry.

Orina stared at him and, as she did, realised what had upset him.

The woman who had walked so far was dead.

To Orina's relief, several people who could hear him crying out in his agony came to see what was happening.

Because they spoke the same language, they were able to commiserate with him.

Orina realised there was nothing she could do.

The man who was guarding her was also there and she said to him:

"I will take the baby back with me. Tell the father so that he will understand where it is."

"Sí, Señora," he replied.

Orina walked back to the steps as quickly as she could with the baby in her arms.

She climbed up them, and it was a relief to find Zeeti was in her cave tidying it.

She told the girl what had happened and said:

"We need milk for the baby."

"No milk, Señora," Zeeti replied.

"Why not?" Orina asked sharply.

"Goats very dear. Como Dios not able afford goats."

Orina was furious.

She wanted to say she thought it selfish of Juarez not to have troubled more about the children.

Then she knew that if she were honest, he had, until he married her, eked out what money he had in the most economical way.

He had to keep the people alive, and at the same time be able to continue his work on the dam.

This meant paying for the tools, the contract, and everything else which was required.

Orina wondered what she could give the baby.

She knew that what was available could not be swallowed by so small a child.

Finally, in desperation, she sent Zeeti to find some honey.

She knew it had come with the last consignment.

It was just one of the small luxuries they were able to afford now that she was paying.

When Zeeti brought it, she mixed it with some water and spooned it into the baby's mouth.

He swallowed a little, then fell asleep in her arms.

She held him close.

Then she told Zeeti to send someone to fetch Juarez.

"*Como Dios* busy on dam," Zeeti said.

"He can leave the dam for a short while," Orina answered.

Zeeti obeyed her and Orina sat nursing the baby.

She was determined that she would save his life.

She knew, now that his mother was dead, she must get milk from somewhere.

"Juarez will arrange it," she told herself. "After all, I have asked for nothing else since I have been here!"

She had given him two more large cheques since she had arrived.

She had not even bothered to read what sum he had written on them.

She had merely signed her name.

She wondered what Bernard Hoffman would think when he was informed by the Bank of the large sums she was withdrawing almost every day.

She knew that a lot of the money was what was required for the materials.

They, too, had arrived surprisingly quickly in wagons drawn by six horses.

"All I want is milk!" Orina said. "And Juarez has to find some for me."

The baby whimpered once or twice, and again she gave him a little spoonful of honey.

"Why is Juarez so long?" she asked angrily. "He must know I would not send for him unless it was important!"

Zeeti brought her a light meal which she ate with one hand so as not to disturb the baby.

Then at last she heard footsteps climbing up the stone steps.

She realised it was now the heat of the day.

The workmen would have stopped for a little while for a *siesta*.

Their wives and children were quiet because they were sheltering from the sun and asleep.

Juarez came into the cave.

"I was told you wanted me," he said curtly.

"You have been a long time in coming!"

"I could not leave before now," he replied. "What is it that you want?"

"I need milk—milk for this baby—his mother is dead."

He looked at her incredulously.

"Milk?" he asked as if he had never heard of it before.

"You need goats, dozens of goats!" Orina said sharply. "But for the moment I must have milk for this child because, as I have told you, his mother cannot feed him because she is dead."

She looked down at the thin little face pressed against her breast.

She had felt since she had been nursing him that she would like to have a baby.

A child of her own—even though she had no wish to be married.

There was something so vulnerable about this tiny boy.

She wanted to protect him and keep him from being hurt or unhappy.

But at the moment, she wanted, above anything else, to feed him.

She was aware that Juarez was staring at her.

She thought perhaps he was angry because in his opinion she had brought him back for a trivial reason.

Unexpectedly, even to herself, she pleaded with him.

"Please," she begged, "please . . . find me some . . . milk with which to . . . feed this poor little boy. I have given him honey, but I can give him nothing else because he is so small."

Without speaking, Juarez moved to stand beside her.

To Orina's surprise, he bent down and took the baby from her arms.

"I am sorry," he said quietly, "but it is too late."

For a moment Orina did not understand.

Then, as she jumped to her feet to look at the baby, she realised what he was saying was true.

The little Spanish boy had died and she had not been aware of it.

Juarez did not speak. He merely went from the cave with the baby in his arms.

He must have given it to the man on guard outside.

When he returned, he was no longer carrying the child.

Orina was standing where he had left her.

"There was nothing you could have done to save him," he said gently.

Something seemed to break within Orina.

Hardly aware of what she was doing, she leaned against him, the tears streaming down her cheeks.

She had her face against his shoulder and he put his arms around her.

"H-he . . . was . . . so small . . . so thin," she sobbed.

"I know," Juarez said, "but after to-morrow, this sort of thing will not happen again."

It took Orina, because she was still crying, a moment to understand what he said.

Then she lifted her face to look up at him.

"You . . . you said . . . to-morrow?" she stammered.

"To-morrow!" Juarez said. "I will also order goats, which I had not thought of before, for the other children. So you see, your Spanish baby did not die in vain."

With an effort Orina wiped her eyes and he took his arms from her.

"I have to go back," he said, "so look after yourself and try not to be unhappy."

She nodded, but she did not speak.

Then Juarez was gone and Zeeti, who was obviously waiting for his departure, came back into the cave.

She made Orina lie down on her bed and prepared some tea.

"To-morrow great day," she said. "Water flowing into dam and everything change. We have water!"

There was a look on her face and an excitement in her eyes.

It told Orina how much it meant to her.

At the same time, she wanted to cry again because the baby was dead.

Neither he nor his mother would see the miracle that would be performed in this barren place.

It suddenly occurred to Orina that if the water flowed as Juarez expected, she would then be free.

The people would grow crops.

The ground would be fertile, as it had been before the earthquake had caused the stream to change direction.

"He will let me go," she told herself.

Then, perhaps because of the baby's death, she did not feel as elated as she thought she would have been.

*   *   *

Juarez came back very late.

In fact, the sun had set and it was almost dark when he arrived.

Dinner had been ready for some time.

Orina had, however, stayed in her own cave in order not to appear to be waiting for him.

It would savour too much, she thought, of a wife traditionally yearning for her husband's return.

Therefore, every evening she had taken care that he was in the large cave just before she joined him.

She heard him go to the shower.

Later there was a sound which told her he was pouring some wine.

Then she thought perhaps it would be the strange clear wine they had drunk on their wedding night.

Ordinarily they had drunk the Mexican wine which came from Ooahuilam in the North and was, she thought, delicious.

Slowly, because she felt a little shy after what had happened earlier in the day, she went into the cave.

He was dressed, as usual, as a *gaucho*, and he turned round as she entered.

"You are all right?" he enquired.

She had not expected him to be concerned.

But it brought back the memory of what she had felt when she realised the baby was dead, so it was impossible to answer him.

She sat alone at her usual place at the table.

He put a beaker of Mexican wine in front of her.

With an effort Orina found her voice.

"I . . . I thought you would be . . . celebrating to-night."

"Not celebrating," he corrected her, "anything may go wrong, so I am crossing my fingers until the last moment."

"The . . . people will be . . . praying."

"And you? What will you be doing?"

She took a sip of the wine before she answered:

"I am . . . expecting," she said at length, "now that I am no longer . . . useful to you, you will be . . . only too . . . willing to be . . . rid of me."

"I suppose that is what I might have expected you to think," he replied.

He sat down opposite her, and Zeeti came hurrying up the steps with a hot dish.

It had been prepared in what was considered the kitchen by one of the women who was a good cook.

It was in a cave that was just below the steps.

Fortunately, any smell and smoke was carried in a different direction so that Orina was not aware of it.

As if it were an effort to please, the food was very much better than usual.

Orina had thought she would not like the very hot spices that accompanied every Mexican dish.

But Juarez had taken the trouble to find somebody who could cook in a different manner from the traditional method.

"Before you came," he told Orina, "I had *masa* every night. I must admit it grew a trifle monotonous."

Now the wagon coming from Sadaro brought chickens, ducks, and, of course, fish from the sea.

It made the evening meal, Orina thought, a delight rather than just a necessity.

Perhaps, because of the expectation of what would happen to-morrow, the food was better than she had ever known it.

While she, however, had little appetite after what had occurred, Juarez ate everything.

She guessed that, as she had sent for him at mid-day, he had in consequence eaten nothing since breakfast.

Only when the last course had been served and Zeeti disappeared did he say:

"Before dinner we were talking about you and you were telling me what you would feel to-morrow. I suppose, to sum it up in one word, it is—free!"

It was exactly what Orina had thought.

At the same time, as she moved her hand she caught a glimpse of her wedding-ring and she said:

"But . . . I am still . . . married."

"In name only," Juarez told her. "I imagine, if you pay the most expensive Lawyers in New York, they will find some easy way of giving you the freedom you so ardently desire."

Because for the moment she did not want to quarrel with him, Orina said:

"I think before anything else, I should congratulate you on what you have achieved. I realise that it is a fantastic undertaking, and if you were in any other country except Mexico, they would certainly show their appreciation by honouring you."

She gave a little laugh before she went on:

"In England they would undoubtedly give you a Knighthood."

"I doubt it," Juarez replied, "and anyway, I do not want one."

"Of course you want to be thanked—everybody does!" Orina argued.

Juarez smiled.

"The people for whom I have built the dam will thank me every time they plough the land, bathe in the stream, and make a *masa* of their own fruits and vegetables."

Orina laughed.

"And while they are doing that, where will you be?"

He made an expressive gesture with his hands.

"I have not yet decided. I came to Mexico to explore the Pyramids and perhaps find some small piece of history that has not yet been discovered."

"If you did discover it, what would you do about it?" Orina persisted.

"Perhaps write a book," Juarez replied, "or else let it be my contribution to posterity."

There was silence, then Orina said:

"That seems rather small and insignificant when you have just achieved something so remarkable as altering the course of a stream, making a dam, and saving the lives of at least a thousand people!"

"And what do you suggest I should do?" Juarez asked.

It was then Orina was aware, almost as if her father were prompting her, that there was a great deal he could do in America.

She held the key to what might almost be termed an Aladdin's Cave of new developments, new ideas, and new productions.

It all passed through her mind.

Then she shrank away from it.

It was hers, and if he were involved, she would not be free of him.

She sat silent, and after a moment he said:

"Exactly! That is why it would be a great mistake for you to suggest it!"

She stared at him in astonishment.

"Are you reading my thoughts?"

"Of course," he replied, "and even if you did make me such a generous offer, I would refuse to accept it."

"Why . . . why should you say that?"

"Because it would involve you! Just as you do not want to be involved with me, I have no wish to be involved with you."

He spoke harshly, and Orina stiffened.

She thought he was being rude.

Then she realised that if he had read her thoughts, it was she who had been rude first.

"When we . . . part," she said, "I think it would be a . . . mistake to do so in an . . . acrimonious manner. All we must really . . . concern ourselves with is that . . . there should be . . . no scandal."

She remembered as she spoke the reason she had run away from New York.

It had been to avoid being involved in a scandal.

It would be very regrettable if she were to be caught up in one here.

"I know what you are thinking," Juarez said, "and we both have to be sensible about this, but, when I have time to give it all my concentration, I am certain I can find a solution, but that will not be until after tomorrow."

Orina laughed because she could not help it.

"Are we really saying this to each other when there has been so much at stake and so much has happened that would seem incredible if we read about it in a book or a newspaper!"

"You are quite right," Juarez replied, "and of course it *is* incredible. But at least we can drink a toast to the miracle of Sadaro. Although it will in the future be a great mistake for us to be involved in it."

"That is not true," Orina cried. "They will never forget you! How could they?"

"And—will you forget me?" Juarez asked.

It was a question she had not expected.

Because he had asked it quietly in his deep voice, she answered truthfully:

"No, it would be . . . impossible for me to . . . forget . . . you."

As she spoke, she knew that was the truth; and it frightened her.

chapter seven

THE tension amongst the people was intense.

Orina could feel it even though she stayed in the cave.

Juarez had told her last night before they went to bed that he was going to open the dam at about four o'clock.

Then it would be cooler.

She had heard him going off to work as soon as it was dawn.

The men who were singing as they went with him had a new lilt in their voices.

She knew this was due to the excitement they were feeling.

Zeeti had a great deal to say when she came in.

"A great day! Only *Como Dios* could bring us water . . . and life!"

Orina knew she was quoting the words of the prayers to Quetzalcoatl.

Then she thought that to-day, of all days, the two religions would be as one.

When the water came into the valley, their lives would be changed.

It was extremely hot at mid-day.

Orina could eat very little of the luncheon which Zeeti brought her.

She thought afterwards she would read for a little while.

She had, although it seemed strange, not done so since she had been a prisoner.

She looked round for books.

As there were none, she went for the first time into Juarez's cave.

It was very like her own with a mattress raised off the floor.

There was beside it a curtain over the clothes that were hung, a roughly-made chest-of-drawers, and two hard chairs.

She looked round.

To her delight, she saw that there were a number of books stacked against one wall.

She looked them over slowly, and found one in English which surprised her.

It was about Mexico, and she thought it was annoying of Juarez not to have suggested she read it before.

She opened the book and turned several of its pages.

It described ancient Mexico and the invasion of the Spaniards in exactly the same way as she had read already.

She read to where a page was turned down and

one word seemed to jump out at her.

"Juarez."

She went from his cave back into her own and sat down on the bed.

This was what she had wanted to know.

In a few pages she learnt why the people below had identified the man building them a dam with a hero.

The real Juarez had been well-educated in a Convent-School, had risen to the Supreme Court, and corresponded with Abraham Lincoln.

Then two sentences seemed to jump out of the page as Orina read them, which said:

He was a great reformer, known for his personal integrity and ideals; a man trying to lead this stumbling country towards a new nationalism.

What Juarez did was to give Mexico a sense of Nationhood.

Orina put down the book.

She was remembering all too vividly her conversations with her father.

At once she thought of Juarez as being like him.

Then she told herself she was being caught up in the excitement of the people outside.

But as far as she was concerned, he had behaved in a very unidealistic manner.

There was more about the real Juarez in the book, but she did not wish to read it.

Instead, she was restless.

She did not sleep through the heat of the day as the women and children were doing outside.

It grew near to the time when Juarez had told her he was going to open the dam.

She put on one of her prettiest gowns.

She laughed at herself for doing so.

She would certainly not be noticed when Juarez was about.

Anyway, he had always made it clear that he was not interested in her as a woman.

'Only as a money-bag!' she thought bitterly.

She picked up her sunshade and walked down the steps.

Her guard smiled at her and she smiled back.

He followed her as she walked into the crowd.

She noticed as she did so that they had divided into two groups.

The Catholics were all seated on the ground behind their Priest.

The others were grouped round the Indian who was wearing the same robes as when he married them.

She positioned herself tactfully between the two groups, and looked up at the mountain.

She could see the new concrete of the dam standing out against the darkness of the grey rocks.

It all looked somehow distant, and for the first time she felt apprehensive.

Suppose, after all their hopes, everything went wrong?

Suppose the stream had run dry or refused to travel in the required direction that Juarez had planned for it?

Therefore, the dam would not fill with water as he had hoped.

There would be nothing to show the people but failure.

Even as she thought of this, she was aware that the people around her were feeling the same.

They did not look so pale or emaciated as they had when she had first come.

The increase in their food had certainly benefitted the children.

At the same time, they were not as healthy as they should be.

She knew it was because they did not have the fresh vegetables from their own land.

The barren earth beneath their feet produced only dust.

Was it really possible that Juarez could change all that?

Again her eyes went to the mountain.

There was no sign of him.

She felt she must call out, ask him to appear and reassure those waiting as well as herself.

Then she saw that the Catholics were saying their rosaries and the Priest was praying.

She looked at the Indian.

Without being able to hear, she knew he was asking Quetzalcoatl for help.

"The God of Rain, the God of Life and of the Morning Star . . ."

No sound came from his lips, but they moved.

All around him the women were also praying silently, not with words, but in their hearts.

It was then, as Orina felt the tension was too

intolerable to be borne, that Juarez appeared.

He was at the side of the dam.

There were several men opposite him on the other side.

She knew what they were going to do and held her breath.

There was no sound from the people, just an awesome silence.

Then she was aware that Juarez was bending over and the man opposite him was doing the same.

They were opening the dam.

Unexpectedly, Orina found herself praying:

"Please . . . God . . . please . . . let there be . . . water! Let it . . . come!"

She felt as if her whole being went into the prayer and came from her soul.

Suddenly there was what seemed like a flash of sunshine.

It was water!

Water pouring out in a glittering stream!

It caught the rays of the sun so that it became an iridescent rainbow which might have come from Heaven itself.

It ran down onto the ground.

It increased in volume until it splashed in the shimmering sunshine.

It was then that Orina knew that tears of relief were running down her cheeks.

It took her a few seconds to be aware that the same thing was happening to those around her.

They did not speak; they did not move.

They just stared at the dazzling stream and

cried from sheer happiness.

As if they were one, the Catholics and the Indians threw up their arms to the sky.

Their voices rang out, thanking God and Quetzalcoatl for giving them the water of life.

It was at that moment that Orina realised she had the answer to the question she had asked before she had come to Mexico.

She had asked if Death was the end or if there was Life after the body had passed away.

Now she knew that her father was beside her, telling her the truth.

There was no such thing as death—Life was Eternal.

He was so vivid to her that she felt she could reach out and touch him.

He was there—and she had found the answer she had sought.

It had come to her as a stream of water pouring down a mountain.

The children broke the tension.

While their parents wept with joy, they ran into the water.

It moved slowly along the dried-up channel where the stream had run in the past.

Some of them must never have seen so much water before in their small lives.

They paddled into it, laughing, shouting, and splashing each other with a joy that was irresistible.

Their mothers wiped away their tears. They went to the side of the stream to bend down and touch the water as if to make sure it was real.

Then they were laughing, but there was a catch in their throats.

Because it was all so emotional, Orina felt she could no longer stay with them.

She wanted to be alone.

She wanted to think about her father coming to her when she least expected it.

She walked back up the steps, aware as she did so that even her guard had forgotten her.

Like all the rest of the people, he was looking at the water.

Some people were touching it and letting it run through their fingers.

Orina did not go into the cave.

She stood on the top step, watching and thinking that the whole scene was a picture.

Any great artist would want to paint it.

It was then that Juarez and his men came down from the mountain.

The people saw him long before he reached the ground.

When they did they prostrated themselves in front of him, and the Indians kissed his feet.

To them he was a God, a God who had brought them life.

The Spaniards kissed his hand and knelt in front of him.

Orina watched as mothers ran to him and asked him to bless their children.

They had been present at a miracle and it would change their lives.

Orina knew that was what they were saying.

Juarez touched the head of one baby after another

before finally he reached the bottom of the steps.

It was then Orina went to her own cave and pulled the curtains over the entrance.

She felt she could not speak to him at this moment.

She could not say how splendid he had been simply because it would make her cry.

She heard him enter the big cave.

She knew he would look round, expecting to find her there.

Then she heard his voice.

"Orina!"

"I am . . . here!" she answered.

There was a silence until he said:

"I will change my clothes and when you are ready we will have dinner."

She guessed as he spoke that he had had nothing to eat since dawn.

She thought, too, that even if food had been there, he would have been too tense to eat.

She was sure the apprehension that something might go wrong at the last moment would have affected him, although, if she spoke of it, he would doubtless deny being anything but calm.

When her father had some big business deal in hand, he would force himself to behave as if it were of little importance.

At the same time, because she loved him, she knew exactly how he was feeling.

She put on a light gown and was not surprised to find there was no Zeeti to help her dress.

How could anyone tear themselves away from the wonder of the stream of life?

She found when she entered the big cave that Juarez was already there.

He was pouring out some of their special wine.

"I think we are entitled to this to-night," he said as she appeared, "and perhaps it is significant that it is the last."

"Significant . . . of what?" Orina asked.

"That my work here is finished, and so is yours," he said quietly. "I will be taking you back to-morrow."

"To-morrow?" Orina repeated.

It had never occurred to her that he would say this to her now.

He poured the wine into the beakers and handed one to her.

"Your yacht is waiting for you," he said, "and you can now resume your voyage—unless you are returning to New York?"

It flashed through Orina's mind that she had thought this would be a Voyage of Discovery.

She had, in fact, discovered perhaps the most important question of all.

Because she was finding it hard to think clearly, she said:

"Are you . . . sending me . . . away . . . or coming . . . with me?"

"I am sending you back to civilisation," Juarez replied. "This was an interlude that was one of necessity. I intend to repay every penny of your money I used. Of course, first I have to obtain employment so that I can make money, so it will take time."

He was speaking once again in his hard,

businesslike voice, the one he had used when he had first brought her to the cave.

She thought of the times they had sat together at dinner.

Then he had discussed and argued with her in a very different tone.

Now she felt insulted, not only by what he said, but also the manner in which he was saying it.

Before, however, she could answer, Zeeti appeared.

She was flushed and apologetic, but she had brought their dinner.

She set it down on the table, saying:

"Forgeeve me . . . forgeeve me! I watch water an' forget time. It wonderful! People say *Como Dios* one great God! They say make statue."

"Thank you," Juarez answered, "but I expect they will remember me without bothering about a statue."

"We make statue!" Zeeti said with determination. "Put on it first of everythin' we grow."

She spoke with such feeling in her voice that Orina found it very touching.

"Thank you, Zeeti," Juarez said again.

The girl went from the cave and Orina said:

"Do you really intend to leave here immediately? Surely they will need you to help them plough, sow, and work the land?"

Juarez shook his head.

"The men who have helped me are all very capable. We have talked about it for a long time, and they have decided exactly what they will do."

"So . . . where will you go?"

He made a gesture with his hands that was very Spanish.

"I have not yet decided," he said. "The world is a very big place."

He was hungry and they did not talk while he was eating.

Orina sat watching him.

She felt as if somebody had suddenly struck her on the head.

It was impossible to think.

The yacht, Captain Bennett, and the voyage they had planned seemed very far away.

New York and London were different worlds.

For a moment it was hard to think of herself as being in either of them.

Zeeti brought in the next course and Juarez poured out some more wine.

When the meal was finished and Zeeti had cleared away the plates and beakers, he said coldly:

"As I now have some packing and other things to attend to, I know you will understand if I leave you. It has been a long day."

"But a very successful one," Orina said quickly.

"Yes, of course," he answered. "Good-night, Orina!"

He left her so abruptly that she felt bewildered.

She wanted to call after him and beg him to stay so that she could talk to him a little longer.

But he was gone and she was too shy to say anything.

She therefore blew out the candles on the table and went to her own cave.

Zeeti had left the candle-lantern alight by her bed.

Slowly Orina undressed.

She could hear the sound of music coming from outside.

The people would be too excited to sleep to-night.

If she was to travel back to-morrow, the sooner she could go to sleep the better.

Otherwise she would find the journey very tiring.

She tried not to think what the people would say when they knew Juarez was going.

She thought they would try to prevent him.

Then she knew he would have an answer to that.

He would doubtless not want any fuss.

She blew out the lantern and settled down to sleep.

But something was wrong, and she was not quite certain what it was.

She was afraid to put into words what she was feeling within herself.

'I should be happy . . . I should be excited at the thought of leaving this place!' she thought.

But somehow nothing seemed real except the moonlight coming through the opening.

It cast a silver light on the floor of the cave.

She must have dozed a little, then awoke with a start.

A strange sound had disturbed her.

It came again, and she thought it was the baying of a dog or the rumbling of falling stones.

It suddenly struck her that it might be an earthquake.

If it was, as had happened before, the stream could once more be diverted.

The people would have no water.

She heard a "boom" "boom" that seemed to her to be coming nearer.

She thought with a feeling of horror that she might be buried alive.

She sprang from her bed as the sound seemed nearer still.

She ran into the big cave.

Without thinking, without questioning, but just as she was, in her thin nightgown and bare feet, she went to Juarez.

She thrust aside the curtain over his cave.

He was in bed, sitting up with a book in his hand, reading by the light of a candle-lantern.

"I . . . I am . . . frightened!" Orina said in a voice that seemed to shake.

"I should have told you," Juarez answered, "it is the wind."

As he spoke, there was an even louder "boom" than there had been before.

Orina did not hear what he said.

With a cry of terror she ran across the cave to fling herself against him.

"Is . . . is it an . . . earthquake?" she whispered.

He dropped his book and put his arms round her.

She stared up at him, her eyes dark with fear,

her hair falling over her shoulders.

For a moment he just stared at her.

"Oh, my God!" he cried.

Then his lips were on hers.

He kissed her wildly, frantically, passionately.

After she had stiffened with shock she did not move.

Then, as his lips possessed her still, she knew that this was what she had been wanting although she had not realised it.

He kissed her and went on kissing her.

He pulled her down beside him so that she was in bed with him.

Their bodies were close against each other's.

To Orina, it was all part of the wonder of the day.

The magic of the flowing water and the nearness of her father.

The emotions of the people were also a part of herself.

She could not think, but only feel an ecstasy which carried her up into the sky.

She had never been kissed, and yet she knew this was just what she should feel, except that it was more rapturous and very much more wonderful.

She felt as if the sunshine which had glistened on the water was moving through her body.

The fire on Juarez's lips was all part of the miracle he had brought down from the mountain.

She was breathless when he raised his head to say hoarsely:

"My darling, my sweet! How can you do this to me?"

Then he was kissing her again, kissing her more demandingly and more passionately.

The fire that she had kindled in him became a burning furnace.

Yet Orina was not afraid.

She only knew that never in her life had she known such wonder, such perfection.

It was part of the Gods to whom she and the people had prayed while they waited for the water to come from the dam.

Then, as if from far away in another world, she heard Juarez say:

"I want you—God how I want you! But my darling—stop me—stop me, for I cannot stop myself!"

There was an appeal in his voice that she did not really understand.

It made her put her arms round his neck and pull him closer to her.

"I love you . . . oh, Juarez . . . I love you . . . I love you!" she whispered.

She thought he gave an exclamation that was one of triumph.

Then, as Juarez made her his, she knew he carried her into Heaven itself.

The wonder and glory of it was the Light of the Morning Star.

*   *   *

A long time later Orina moved against Juarez's shoulder.

She felt his arms immediately tighten around her.

"Forgive me," he said, "I did not mean this to happen."

"But . . . I love you," Orina replied, "and I know now I have . . . loved you for a very long time . . . or perhaps it was only hours . . . I knew it . . . but I could not put it into words . . . when you opened the dam and the water came flooding down onto the barren ground."

"I have loved you since the moment I first saw you," Juarez answered. "I did not believe anyone could be so beautiful, but I tried to tell myself that all I wanted was your money."

"And now . . . you love me . . . because I am . . . me?" Orina asked.

"I love you as I never imagined I could love anyone," Juarez answered, "but because I have nothing to offer you, my precious one, I must give you freedom to go away."

Orina gave a cry of horror.

"Go? Go away . . . now that I . . . belong to you? How can you think of . . . anything so cruel?"

Juarez's arms tightened for a moment. Then he said:

"I did not mean to make love to you. I intended to take you back to your yacht to-morrow—or is it to-day—then disappear."

"But . . . but you cannot! You cannot do . . . anything so . . . wicked . . . so cruel!"

"I have to," he said, "for my own self-respect."

Orina gave a cry of horror.

"Papa once said that most . . . Englishmen

149

would . . . not want to marry me . . . because of my money . . . and I found the men who . . . proposed to me . . . wanted me only for what I . . . could give them."

There was a note of cynicism in her voice that made Juarez ask tentatively:

"Is that why you said you hated men?"

Orina nodded and turned her face against his shoulder.

"Tell me what happened," he said.

"It was . . . when I was in England . . . when I was . . . first a debutante."

He kissed her hair as she went on:

"There was one man . . . he was a Marquis . . . and very good-looking. Because he paid me a . . . great deal of attention . . . I believed he was . . . in love with me."

"But you found he was not?" Juarez asked.

"I overheard a conversation just as I was entering a room between him and another man called Henry."

Orina drew in her breath as if it were still a painful memory and went on:

"I heard Henry say: 'You are obviously very taken with Orina Vandeholt! Are you thinking of marrying her?'

"The Marquis laughed.

" 'Great Heavens, no! Can you imagine what my family's reaction would be if I married an American?'

"Then Henry replied," Orina said:

" 'She is a rather exceptional American! Her father is the richest man in the whole country, and likely to become even richer!' "

Orina shut her eyes.

It was still agonising for her to remember what the Marquis had said.

Yet somehow she forced herself to repeat it.

" 'I had no idea of that,' he exclaimed, 'and for that amount of money I would marry an Indian Squaw!' "

Juarez put his fingers under her chin and lifted her face up to his.

"So you thought all men were like that!"

"Yes—Englishmen as well as Americans—I could almost see them . . . counting my millions before . . . asking me if I would be their . . . wife!"

"My poor darling," Juarez said. "I can understand exactly what you felt. At the same time, as an Englishman, I want you to be my wife, but it will take me many years to be able to keep you in the manner to which you are accustomed, and that is why I have to go away."

"If you do," Orina warned, "I shall follow you. I will . . . live in a tent, in a hut, a cave! I will not spend one cent of my own . . . money, and if we starve—we starve . . . together."

Juarez stared at her as if he could not believe what he was hearing.

"Do you mean that?" he asked.

"I swear to you on . . . everything I hold . . . sacred that I am . . . speaking the . . . truth!"

Juarez pulled her so close to him that she could hardly breathe.

"Can you really love me as much as that?" he asked.

"More . . . much . . . much . . . more," Orina whispered, "but you will have to . . . show me how you can . . . dispose of all the things Papa . . . acquired because he . . . believed that development and production would help his country."

Juarez did not speak, and she went on:

"I was reading to-night how your . . . namesake . . . the great Reformer . . . gave Mexico a sense of Nationhood. That is what Papa believed he was doing in America."

Juarez was silent, as if he were thinking.

"We cannot leave all . . . those things like . . . a ship without a rudder," Orina went on. "We must put the right men in the . . . right places. Some of them . . . will grow old and have to be . . . replaced. A few will . . . invariably . . . fail and somebody will have . . . to find . . . a substitute."

She looked up at him.

"Help me . . . please . . . help me to do what is right . . . but I am your . . . wife and I will not . . . leave you."

Juarez still did not speak.

Now, frantically, in case she lost him, she was thinking as her father had taught her to do—reasonably, logically, and intelligently.

How could she induce him to stay with her?

Finally, in a small voice he could hardly hear, she asked:

"D-do you think . . . perhaps you have . . . given me a . . . b-baby?"

She felt Juarez stiffen before he said:

"I tried to stop myself! It was wrong—of course it was wrong—to make you mine. But I could no

152

longer control myself as I have done every night while we slept with a cave between us."

"You . . . wanted me . . . you really . . . wanted me?" Orina asked.

"Unbearably!" he said. "You are far too beautiful, my precious, for any man's peace of mind!"

He touched her body gently.

Then, as she queried, he said:

"I am ashamed of myself for being so weak and having so little self-control."

"I think what . . . you are . . . really saying is . . . that you are . . . sorry you . . . love me," Orina answered miserably.

"No, no, that is not true!" he contradicted her. "I love you because you are so brave and behaved so well in what I realise was an intolerable situation."

"But now . . . you want to . . . leave me! Oh, Juarez . . . how can you be so cruel?"

Again he was silent and she said:

"Suppose I have . . . a baby and . . . because you are . . . not there it . . . dies like that poor . . . little Spanish baby . . . died without its mother?"

"You are not to think of such things," Juarez said sharply. "There is no real reason to assume that you should have a baby the first time I make love to you."

"I shall . . . pray that I . . . do have . . . one," Orina said, "but . . . please . . . Juarez . . . it would be . . . frightening to have one if I am all . . . alone, however many . . . doctors, nurses, and other tiresome people there are . . . fussing over . . . me."

"You are tempting me," Juarez said, "and all I can say is that I am deeply in your debt, and somehow I have to repay you before I can feel I am a man again."

"Does . . . money really . . . matter to you . . . more than . . . love?" Orina asked.

There was no answer, and after a moment she said:

"Very well . . . if you . . . leave me I shall . . . follow you, and . . . wherever you go I will go. If all the things Papa built up in his . . . lifetime . . . crash, or are . . . ruined through . . . sheer inefficiency . . . there will be . . . nothing I can . . . do . . . about it."

The last words were a little sob.

Then Juarez said:

"Adam was right when he said that Eve tempted him!"

Then he was kissing her again, kissing her wildly and fiercely as he had done at first.

Yet Orina knew it was different.

He was asserting himself as a man, being dominating, possessive, and forcing her to surrender.

Then, as she was aware that the ecstasy rising in her body and her mind and her heart was echoed in him, she knew that he would not leave her.

* * *

They reached the yacht the following afternoon when the sun had lost its heat.

At the same time, it had been a long ride and a tiring one.

They had stopped for luncheon at the same farm where Orina had eaten before.

Juarez insisted they rest on one of the mattresses which he pulled down from the pile onto the floor.

They knew they would not be disturbed by the Indian woman who was in the kitchen.

As Juarez made love to her, Orina knew that this time she would not be drugged, except with happiness.

They reached Sadaro.

The story of what had happened at the dam had, in some magical way, already been carried on the wind.

People ran out of their dilapidated houses to cheer Juarez.

A whole crowd of children looked at Orina with pleading eyes.

She and Juarez rode to the Quay.

Then they dismounted. Orina gave them what coins she had left in her pockets.

She told them to go and buy some fruit for themselves.

Jumping for joy, they obeyed her.

As they did so, Orina looked apprehensively at Juarez.

She was afraid he might think that she was throwing her money about.

She could not help feeling that it was going to be very difficult in the future.

Daily, if not hour by hour and minute by minute, they might contrast the difference between them.

Captain Bennett greeted them and they went into the Saloon.

"I have ordered refreshment and particularly something cool to drink," he said. "Dinner will be served a little later."

"Thank you, Captain," Orina replied. "I expect you have heard that I am married."

"I have indeed," the Captain replied, "and I hope that you will be very, very happy."

He turned to Juarez.

"My congratulations to you, Sir! And may I add that I am extremely impressed by your amazing achievement!"

He gave a short laugh before he added:

"I do not think anyone in Sadaro has ever thought of turning the direction of the stream before!"

Juarez smiled, but he did not say anything, and the Captain went on:

"By the way, Sir, I have here a telegram which I understand from Father Miguel is for you. They were wondering at Government House for whom it could be, not knowing your name was Mr. Standish."

He handed over the telegram as he spoke.

Orina wondered nervously what it contained.

As the Captain left the Saloon, Juarez stood looking at it and she asked:

"What does it . . . say? I did not know . . . anyone knew you . . . were here!"

"It comes from New York," he answered.

Because she was curious, she went close to him, thinking it could not be bad news.

If it was, perhaps he would be more reluctant than ever to do what she wanted.

Without asking his permission Orina read the telegram over his shoulder.

It was addressed to: Alexis Standish, Esq., c/o Government House Sadaro.

FROM MILTON RIDGEWORTH ASSISTANT TO HIS EXCELLENCY THE AMBASSADOR BRITISH EMBASSY NEW YORK STOP DEEPLY REGRET INFORM YOU YOUR UNCLE LORD STANDISH OF BROADWAY BRITISH AMBASSADOR TO USA DIED TODAY OF HEART ATTACK STOP PLEASE RETURN NEW YORK AS SOON AS POSSIBLE STOP NEED YOU TO ARRANGE BODY CONVEYED FOR BURIAL AS INSTRUCTED IN WILL.

Orina read it slowly. Then she said:

"I had no idea that your uncle was the British Ambassador! I think Papa must have known him."

"I am sure he did," Juarez answered, "and, of course, my darling, you realise this changes things considerably."

Orina was frightened.

"B-but . . . why? What do you . . . mean?"

"I am my uncle's heir," Juarez said, "and I must escort his body back to England for interment in the family vault."

He saw the question in Orina's eyes, and added:

"You will, of course, come with me, and naturally I want you to see the house which will now be mine, and in which we will stay some months of the year, even though we must spend the rest of the time coping with your father's possessions in America."

For a moment Orina could not believe what he was saying.

Then she asked a little incoherently:

"Are . . . are you saying . . . that your uncle has . . . left you . . . his money?"

Juarez smiled.

"He has left me enough to keep my wife in comfort," he said, "and also, I think she will enjoy having a title."

"I do not . . . believe . . . it!" Orina said. "Oh, Juarez . . . I do not . . . believe this is . . . happening."

The tears were back in her eyes.

As she put her arms round his neck, she whispered:

"I knew Papa was . . . helping me when I felt him . . . beside me as you . . . opened the . . . dam. I know . . . now he must have . . . chosen you long . . . before I . . . did to be my husband and to . . . look after his . . . Empire."

"We will make it great, my precious," Juarez said, "not only for America, but also for England. Our two countries, who speak the same language, must be a part of each other."

"Of course . . . of course!" Orina agreed. "And my darling, wonderful husband, I am a . . . part of . . . you and now you . . . will not . . . try to get . . . rid of . . . me?"

Juarez held her very close.

"That is something I am quite certain I would never have been able to do," he said, "but now I can be your husband and hold my head high!"

"I do not . . . care how high you hold your . . . head as long as . . . you make quite . . . certain that what is . . . yours is mine, and what is . . . mine is . . . yours!"

"I will do that!" Juarez promised.

He held her closer still.

He was kissing her in a way that told her that the last cloud had rolled away.

Now their love was as perfect as they wanted it to be.

It was a love that would, she knew, increase year by year because it came from a Miracle and was part of a Miracle.

Shining over them there was the Light of God and the Light of the Morning Star.

Barbara Cartland, the world's most famous romantic novelist, who is also an historian, playwright, lecturer, political speaker and television personality, has now written over 540 books and sold over 500 million copies all over the world.

She has also had many historical works published and has written four autobiographies as well as the biographies of her mother and that of her brother, Ronald Cartland, who was the first Member of Parliament to be killed in the last war. This book has a preface by Sir Winston Churchill and has just been republished with an introduction by Sir Arthur Bryant.

Love at the Helm, a novel written with the help and inspiration of the late Earl Mountbatten of Burma, Great Uncle of His Royal Highness The Prince of Wales, is being sold for the Mountbatten Memorial Trust.

She has broken the world record for the last fourteen years by writing an average of twenty-three books a year. In the *Guinness Book of Records* she is listed as the world's top-selling author.

Miss Cartland in 1978 sang an Album of Love Songs with the Royal Philharmonic Orchestra.

In private life Barbara Cartland, who is a Dame of the Order of St. John of Jerusalem, Chairman of the St. John Council in Hertfordshire and Deputy

President of the St. John Ambulance Brigade, has fought for better conditions and salaries for Midwives and Nurses.

She championed the cause for the Elderly in 1956 invoking a Government Enquiry into the "Housing and Conditions of Old People."

In 1962 she had the Law of England changed so that Local Authorities had to provide camps for their own Gypsies. This has meant that since then thousands and thousands of Gypsy children have been able to go to School, which they had never been able to do in the past, as their caravans were moved every twenty-four hours by the Police.

There are now fourteen camps in Hertfordshire and Barbara Cartland has her own Romany Gypsy Camp called Barbaraville by the Gypsies.

Her designs "Decorating with Love" were sold all over the U.S.A. and the National Home Fashions League made her, in 1981, "Woman of Achievement."

She is unique in that she was one and two in the Dalton list of Best Sellers, and one week had four books in the top twenty.

Barbara Cartland's book *Getting Older, Growing Younger* has been published in Great Britain and the U.S.A. and her fifth cookery book, *The Romance of Food*, is now being used by the House of Commons.

In 1984 she received at Kennedy Airport America's Bishop Wright Air Industry Award for her contribution to the development of aviation. In 1931 she and two R.A.F. Officers thought of, and carried, the first aeroplane-towed glider airmail.

During the War she was Chief Lady Welfare Officer in Bedfordshire looking after 20,000 Service men and women. She thought of having a pool of Wedding Dresses at the War Office so a Service Bride could hire a gown for the day.

She bought 1,000 gowns without coupons for the A.T.S., the W.A.A.F's and the W.R.E.N.S. In 1945 Barbara Cartland received the Certificate of Merit from Eastern Command.

In 1964 Barbara Cartland founded the National Association for Health of which she is the President, as a front for all the Health Stores and for any product made as alternative medicine.

This is now a £650,000 turnover a year, with one third going in export.

In January 1988 she received *La Médaille de Vermeil de la Ville de Paris*. This is the highest award to be given in France by the City of Paris for achievement—25 million books sold in France.

In March 1988 Barbara Cartland was asked by the Indian Government to open their Health Resort outside Delhi. This is almost the largest Health Resort in the world.

Barbara Cartland was received with great enthusiasm by her fans, who fêted her at a reception in the City, and she received the gift of an embossed plate from the Government.

Barbara Cartland was made a Dame of the Order of the British Empire in the 1991 New Year's Honours List by Her Majesty The Queen for her contribution to literature and also her work for the community.